I0685753

DAUGHTERS of a DARK FAIRY

NIKI LIVINGSTON

DAUGHTERS OF A DARK FAIRY

Copyright © 2025 Niki Livingston

Publisher: Unbound Wonders Press

Editor: Novel Nurse Editing

Book cover design by © GetCovers.com

ISBN-13: 978-1-952537-20-2

To connect: www.NikiLivingston.com

DAUGHTERS of a DARK FAIRY

To those who have survived the storm of narcissistic abuse.
I see you.
I know what it takes to untangle yourself from what felt like love but was really control, confusion, and hurt dressed up as charm.
This is for your strength, your softness, and your courage.
You didn't imagine it. You weren't too sensitive. You were surviving.
And you are so worthy of real love, especially your own.

PROLOGUE

Paislee

The thick fog swallowed me as I raced barefoot through the trees, avoiding the path Ryker's men were guarding. My heavy breathing betrayed me, but I refused to shift before I was ready to fight my sister again. I had been running from them for hours, and still I couldn't talk myself into the required transformation.

It was all a twisted game, Ryker's rules—a method to tighten our grip over our demons by turning us against each other as prey—but it always felt like he was preparing us for something far more sinister. My demon had grown stronger, more formidable, and the gleam in Ryker's eyes said everything. He relished the chaos and the inevitable end it promised.

Pandora's croaky cries followed close behind me, begging for a fight that would end with her bruised and beaten. She yearned to please Ryker. But me—I wished for escape and to never see the man again.

"Paislee, show me your demon." Ryker's booming voice traveled through the vegetation, despite him not being within the forest.

His voice echoed through the trees, and the soundwaves struck me with a force that chilled me to the bone. There was no fleeing from him, no shelter from the shadow that clung to his presence. The truth mocked me with its silence. Mom and Mimi spoke only in riddles, their words woven with fear and something older, something wrong. Their refusal to leave had sealed our fate, binding us to this place.

But my wish hung over me, heavy on my mind.

His tone carried his irritation at my delay. I needed more time. Pandora would suffer if I made the wrong move, and if I caused her any more pain, I would never forgive myself.

The sound of a flap of wings caught my attention, and I skidded to a halt, sliding behind a wide tree trunk to obscure my whereabouts. I peeked around the tree and scanned the branches for Pandora. She settled on a tree branch across from me and stared pointedly at me. I never could throw her off my trail.

I waved her away. "Give me five minutes. Please. I'm almost ready."

Pandora's feathers ruffled, then she turned her back toward me, cawing in the direction we had come. Her curved beak snapped shut, and she twisted her neck to side-eye me, then unfurled her wings. They expanded the length of the branch. Pandora's raven form was massive compared to others of her kind, but not large enough to defeat me.

I hated this helplessness, and I wanted to shake her for submitting to him so easily. "Seriously, Dora?" I grumbled before sprinting away from her again.

Thorns and small sticks dug into the bottoms of my feet, but I did my best to ignore their sting and picked up my speed. I traversed the thick brush, scratching and cutting my arms and legs before finding a small cove surrounded by close grown trees.

I whirled in a circle, making sure I hadn't been seen. The branches folded in closer to me and closed the gaps between the trunks to shield me. I blew out a shaky breath and leaned against one of the trees, gratitude for their protection warming my chest.

"Thank you," I whispered as I trailed my fingers along the bark of the nearest branch.

I slid down the trunk and sat on the moss covering, allowing the energy from the earth to recharge me. It flowed steadily through my limbs, reminding me of what Mom had told me when I was younger.

Our protection comes from our connection to nature. Ryker's control may feel all-consuming, but we have the power to tap into Mother Earth's energy. As women, we are the portal for life, and he knows we outnumber him. Between us and nature, we will always be more powerful than him.

The forest remained my sanctuary, but tapping into my own power without Ryker using it to his advantage seemed impossible.

"She went this way," a man yelled from just beyond the circle of trees.

I dug my fingers into the dirt, sending my wish through the earth. "Please," I whispered. My mind raced as visions of another life outside of this hell swirled in my mind.

A sudden, uncontrollable surge of adrenaline overcame me, and my limbs trembled from the energy. I leaped to my feet. The branches around me shifted, revealing a gap on the opposite side from the approaching voices. I crawled through and burst into a sprint, zigzagging through the vegetation and hurdling over fallen trees in my way without a glance behind me.

Their clamorous footsteps were closing the distance. I pressed forward, using the roaring terror in my ears to pump my arms and legs faster.

To my left, a sparkle of light flashed and caught my attention. I veered in that direction, hope rising in my chest. I had made it to the field on the other side of the forest. In my seventeen years, I had never ventured this far, and every muscle screamed at me to keep going.

"This way!" a man hollered, closing in on me.

The glimmer brightened, and I focused on its beacon, swerving around another large tree and a clump of bushes. The branches cracked and groaned as the vegetation bent to slow the pursuit of the men behind me.

I burst through the thickest area of the forest and stumbled into a clearing. The sun beat down on me, but it wasn't the light I had been following.

Feet in front of me, a slit of illumination sparkled. It appeared as if there were a rift in the air itself, which crackled along its edges, widening to reveal a different field on the other side. It brightened as if to beckon me to approach.

The sound of breaking branches had me inching closer to the light.

"What is that?" a man yelled.

I glanced over my shoulder and found two men tangled in the vegetation, staring at the illumination in horror. Vines had weaved around their limbs and tightened with each movement. The men's gazes darted between me and the light as they wrestled against the hold.

My attention returned to the crack in the air, and I reached for it, allowing my fingers to glide through the sparkling radiance. They appeared on the other side as if it were a doorway and nothing else. I gulped and took another step forward, brushing my toes through it.

"He will find you. Don't go any farther!" one of the men hollered from his tangled entrapment.

Worry gnawed at me, fearing he spoke the truth. But wasn't this the opportunity I had wished for? I stole one last glance behind me, hoping to see Pandora, but she had vanished.

"I will strangle you myself." One man freed his arm that held a dagger. He sawed at the limb wrapped around his other arm.

His threat lit a fire underneath me, giving me all the motivation I needed. I leaped through the crack and to the ground on the other side, then rolled down a steep incline. I wrapped my arms around my head as rocks and dirt scratched against my skin, digging into my back and thighs. The world spun above me and a cry burst from my lips when I grazed a large boulder and it ripped my pants down the side, taking inches of my flesh with it.

The fall stretched for several long seconds before I slid to halt on my back and stared up at the cloudless sky.

My breath came in sharply as I shot to my feet. Pain radiated down my thigh as I whirled in a circle, searching for the light. It sparked and crackled like a fire several yards up the hill. I raced toward it, kicking up pebbles and cursing as I slid backward time and again when the incline was steeper than I'd anticipated.

My chest tightened like a vise, each breath shallow and

sharp, scraping against my throat. I couldn't leave Pandora behind. As I grew closer to the ebbing light, it flickered and sparked again before disappearing entirely.

ONE

Paislee

I jolted upright in the hotel bed. Light filtered around the edges of the blackout curtains, reminding me I had left my one-bedroom apartment the day before and was returning to my childhood home today.

Ten. Years. I already missed my bed and quiet apartment above the garage of my coworker's parents' house.

Pandora's email had come out of nowhere, after a full decade of no contact. I had almost forgotten my family existed until I'd read her bleak words.

I squirmed to the edge of the bed, reluctant to make this my last morning outside of the property that had held me for the first seventeen years of my life. But it was time to face the fire. Literally. I blew out a long breath and hurried to the bathroom.

After dressing in jeans and a white shirt, I packed up my belongings and closed the door to my hotel room.

One man stood in the corner of the elevator when I entered, but thankfully, he didn't acknowledge my entrance. On the next floor, another middle-aged man walked in, but his face lit up when he saw me.

Ten floors to the garage. I gritted my teeth.

The black grime on the edges of the elevator floor captured my full attention as we descended. The newest member to the elevator stood in the middle, and I noticed his feet turn slightly toward me when he spoke. It took me a few seconds to comprehend his words as I did everything I could to not look at him.

His voice echoed in the small space, oblivious to my nervous energy. "And I told the maid that this time she better do a thorough cleaning. I have a long day ahead of me, and dust on my nightstand is unacceptable. Where would I place my phone and laptop if they don't keep the surfaces cleaned?" He sighed heavily. "You know what I mean? This hotel is supposed to be a five-star experience, not a one-star dump."

He tapped me on the shoulder, and I cringed. My chest tightened with fear, and I shot him a startled look. He had already turned away from me and was continuing with his story while my mind drowned his voice out with my own

2

frightened thoughts.

Ten fucking years. Home wasn't where I wanted to be, but here I was, making the drive despite my heart warning me to run in the opposite direction.

For Mimi. Right?

The other man shifted but never looked our way. When I glanced at him, a black shimmer above his head caught my eye. I squinted at it, but it disappeared as quickly as it came. I rubbed my eyes and gave the descending floor light buttons my full attention.

I should have taken the stairs. I hated elevators, and even after all these years, I despised being alone with men. But my luggage weight had convinced me to ignore my intuition.

"Am I right or am I right?" The man telling the story laughed and then blew out another breath. "It's going to be a good day. I'm invested in this new project of mine after having too many years with the boss's boot on my—"

The elevator jolted to a stop and my focus darted to the doors.

"Man, they need to fix this elevator. A bit of bumpy rice, don't you think? One time I was staying in New York, and the elevator broke down while I was inside."

Sweat beaded on my brow, but I quickly swiped it

away with the back of my arm. The doors were not opening, but the light indicated we had reached the parking garage.

"And I screamed against the opening of the door, praying someone would hear me. The call button would not work, and my phone had no bars. I thought I was going to die in there."

My cheeks burned with dread. Did he ever shut up? I envisioned his charred body seared to the wall of the elevator, steam wafting from his core. Heat surged in my veins, swimming relentlessly toward my heart.

No! Not this. Anything but this.

I clenched my fists, shoving the dreadful image from my mind. My intrusive thoughts were my downfall—and one of the many reasons I had stayed away from my family for so long. I lightly tapped the sides of my thighs, focusing on my therapist's advice from years before.

Gag them. Silence his voice. Your family's voices. But especially his. You are in control, and he no longer has any power over you.

The panic dissipated after a few controlled breaths, and I refocused on the problem in front of me. The elevator doors remained shut. I jammed on the parking garage button several times. Nothing happened.

"That won't help, honey." He chuckled and continued

4

with his story. "But then I heard a faint voice from the other side. I was in between floors, so it was coming from above me."

My rage resurfaced like a burst of light inside my chest. I pried my gaze off the elevator buttons and turned my attention to the talkative, blue-eyed man. Instead, the black shimmer above the other man's head took my focus. He glanced my way and took a quick sudden step back when he noticed my gaze. A shocked expression melted down his face as we stared in horror at one another.

There was something eerily familiar about him.

The elevator beeped, and the doors grunted as they opened. I swallowed hard and bolted through the welcomed opening, not thinking about the direction of my car. It didn't matter. That suffocating feeling began to subside as soon as I had put some distance between me and the men.

I had been dreading this day for weeks. Being stuck in the elevator for even a few minutes reminded me of the life I had escaped. The familiar sense of anxiety hit way too close to my heart.

But Pandora had promised. No one controlled my family anymore. I could safely return home without the threat of reimprisonment looming over me.

The bumper of my Honda Civic caught my eye, and I

jogged toward it.

"Hey! You dropped your keys."

The storytelling man's voice stopped me in my tracks. I whirled around, and sure enough, he was holding up my purple rabbit's foot key ring. Flames licked the insides of my throat, and my guts curdled with embarrassment as I walked toward him.

"You really should be more careful." He stared hard at me as if he wanted to say more.

"Thank you," I mumbled with a curt nod.

I took my keys and backed away.

The quiet man from the elevator appeared behind him and walked past the storyteller, pinning me with his stare. "There is a good lesson to take from his story."

The storyteller nodded at me and turned in the other direction, ignoring the taller man as he passed us. I turned to watch the man with the shimmering black halo above his head, mesmerized by his entire aura.

He threw me a quick glance as if making sure I was listening. "Sometimes, circumstances arise in our lives to warn us to proceed with caution or pivot entirely. Pay attention, and choose your next steps wisely." He rounded the next corner without another glance and disappeared from sight.

My heart hammered against my chest. "Odd," I

6

muttered under my breath after I was sure he was out of hearing range.

I unlocked my car door and slid into the front seat with a long sigh whistling between my lips. I didn't want to go. But if I didn't show up to say good-bye, I would never forgive myself. Too much had happened, and the longer I waited, the worse it would become.

I missed Mom and Pandora, but Mimi had been my confidant and closest friend. If her end was near, I owed her a visit, and with Ryker out of the picture, there wasn't a reason to stay away.

My Honda Civic purred to life with a twist of the key. Flying would have been faster, but I didn't want to chance being seen—not after suppressing that side of me for ten years and doing everything in my power to tame the demon inside.

The parking garage disappeared from my rearview mirror when I turned the corner and made my way to the freeway.

Ten years had been long enough to bury the horrors of the home I had grown up in, but my memories were resurfacing, jagged and persistent, like something buried alive. Ryker's hold on my family had always been shrouded in mystery, a presence that twisted itself around us until we stopped noticing the choke. He had called

7

himself our guardian, and residing at his estate had come with strict adherence to his rules, but it was the only life I had known. I had accepted it because I had to.

Growing up with invisible chains makes freedom a cruel tale told to mock the broken.

How I'd escaped was a fuzzy memory I couldn't quite piece together. But I remember the road to return home like I had driven it yesterday.

Trauma has a way of peeling away the better parts of you and leaving a shell of a person behind, even after a decade of healing.

As I stopped at the first red light, I glanced at the car next to me. The quiet man from the elevator stared back at me from the passenger seat. A woman sang and swayed to unheard music in the driver's seat, paying no attention to her passenger. Curiosity swept across his gaze, and familiarity clawed at my heart, but I could not place his face. It chilled me to the bone.

Who are you? I mouthed at the man.

Someone behind me honked, and I jumped, my gaze snapping to the green light. I white-knuckled the steering wheel, but before pressing the gas, I quickly glanced over again. The car with the man in it was speeding off down the road to my left.

Goose bumps traveled down my back. I moved

through the light at a snail's pace, ignoring the honking behind me as I tried to place the man's face. My memory came up empty, but his words echoed in my mind.

Sometimes, circumstances arise in our lives to warn us to proceed with caution or pivot entirely. Pay attention, and choose your next steps wisely.

TWO

Pandora

My feet crunched against the dry leaves as I walked along the forest path, inhaling a deep breath after spending the morning among the trees. The day had finally arrived, and I felt Paislee growing closer. It was a twin thing. I sensed her before I heard her car pull into the long driveway.

Jealousy curled through my ribs, and I clenched my jaw to ward away the feeling.

Nearby tree branches folded toward me. I patted them as I passed by. "Yes, she's coming. It will be just like when we were younger. I'll have her visit you soon."

They missed Paislee. I did too. But I despised her more.

I wiped my hands down the long length of my obsidian hair and smoothed down any stray locks. Several leaves fell from my shoulders and fluttered to the earth. My long visit to the forest usually resulted in a few remnants. A grin stretched my cheeks, and I twirled in a circle, joy warming me from within as I pushed any other feelings into the farthest, darkest areas of my mind. It really was a good day.

Soon I could put all of this behind me, and my internal conflict would be a thing of history.

The shadows folded away from me when I stepped into the sun and left the trees behind. The estate loomed in front of me with the tall beams showcasing the front entrance as each side stretched the length of a football field or more in each direction. The corner stones wrapped the edges, giving definition and character to the sad, old place.

Home. It was the only one I had known, and I hated every inch of it.

The sound of Paislee's car grew nearer, which meant she had reached the property boundaries. My gaze drifted to the hillside that stood between the estate and the closest town, and I noticed a slight swirl of dust from an approaching car. There was no turning back now.

Anticipation bubbled in my stomach, and I tore toward the estate, swerving around the cars and staff arriving for the day.

"She's here," I sang, bursting through the side door near the kitchen.

11

Most of the kitchen staff ignored me, but a few jumped from my boisterous entrance. I skipped around them to find Mimi in the dining room. I planted a sloppy kiss on her forehead.

Her green eyes lit up. "Who's here, dear?" She wiped her mouth with her napkin and leaned back with curiosity.

"Paislee. We are having a proper family reunion this weekend." I ran my hands along her hair and tucked her locks behind her ears.

Mimi's expression crumbled, and she dropped her napkin to her lap. "You didn't, Pandora. Please tell me you're teasing. How did you even find her?"

"Ye of little faith, Mimi. I told you I would find her, and neither of you believed me. Besides, I would never tease about seeing my sister again. We have missed her so much. Are you not thrilled?" I bopped her on the nose and twirled away from her, leaving the room without waiting for an answer.

The crunch of tires on the rocks out front had me racing across the marble floor of the entryway. I skidded to a halt at the door and smoothed my hair down one last time. I threw open the door and rushed out to Paislee.

Her Honda Civic stopped a few feet from me, and through the windshield, my sister stared back. I waved, excitement bursting inside me to the point I thought I

12

would explode with happiness. Finally.

She climbed out of the car and raised her brows. "Is it really safe, Dora?"

Her dark-brown eyes and black hair matched mine. Aside from a spattering of freckles on her nose and a slightly tanned complexion, we were identical in every way. Elation coursed through me. I had missed her, even though she had abandoned me. We were supposed to conquer this world together, but instead I had been left to pick up the pieces of her disappearance.

"Yes, Pais," I replied in a sickly-sweet tone, skipping to her and throwing my arms around her neck. "It has been too long. Why haven't you visited?"

"It's complicated." She squeezed me, then dropped her arms and pulled away. Her gaze darted around the landscape as if she was searching for an escape. "I had forgotten how stifling this place had been."

"Silly girl." I swatted her arm playfully. "Grab your things and come see Mom. You have nothing to worry about. You never did."

I shooed her forward and into the house, giving the forest a sideways glance. This had to be done. The trees would forgive me someday. Their branches stretched toward us, but Paislee's attention had already been captured by what she found inside.

"Where is she?" Paislee's gaze traveled the length of the massive entryway as if she were searching every corner for the boogeyman.

I giggled at her paranoia and waved at the staircase. "In her art room. She's going to be delighted to see you after all these years." I enunciated the last few words, wanting to lay on the guilt as heavily as possible.

She'd abandoned me. Paislee did not deserve anything but the worst from here on out. I shoved away the glimmer of shame prickling my scalp and buried it with cement in the darkest recesses of my mind, with my other distracting emotions.

Paislee stepped gingerly onto the first step, worry etched across her expression. I ignored it. If she couldn't trust me, her own twin, then to hell with her. She was here, and that was all that mattered.

"I want to see Mimi. Is she in her suite?"

"No." I slipped my hand in hers and squeezed it, encouraging her with our twin connection. I chuckled internally at her grateful smile. "But I will take you to her next."

She nodded, satisfied with my answer. She was now a stranger to this home, hesitant to explore like we had as children. I could use this to my advantage.

We walked in silence to the third floor. Paislee twirled

in a circle at the top, like we had done when we were young, and a small smile teased the edges of her lips.

"Forgetting this place had been too easy." She thrust out her hips to the right and used it to prop up her bag. "I hadn't realized how much I missed you until just now. We were dealt an awful hand with Ryker's hunts, but the fun we had when he was away or preoccupied with business…" She laughed, dropped her bags to the floor, and twirled again like a princess in a dress. "I missed you, Pandora."

Guilt coiled through my insides, but I forced a bright smile. "I'm happy you're home." I waved her forward. "Mom will feel the same way."

She swung her bag back into her arms and walked beside me to the back of the house, where Mom had her art room. It was tucked in a corner, away from the hustle and bustle, where she could focus without interruption.

Paislee stopped short a few feet before the door. "I saw a strange man today who looked awfully familiar. He said something that has me second-guessing—"

"Who cares what a stranger said to you?" I grabbed her arm and gave her an encouraging squeeze. The anticipation of seeing Mom's face was tearing apart my insides. "You're here now. Let's not waste another minute."

She worried her bottom lip, fiddling with her luggage before setting it down again. Then she tapped quietly on the door.

I felt giddy with happiness.

"Come in, Dora. You know you don't have to knock," Mom called from the other side.

"Didn't she know I was coming?" Paislee turned the knob and opened the door before I could answer. "Hey, Mom." Her worried expression melted away, and a grin blossomed on her face when Mom turned her way.

Mom's eyes widened, and a look of horror overtook her face. Her gaze shot to mine. "Dora, what have you done?"

THREE

Paislee

Confused from Mom's reaction, I shot a look at Pandora, searching for an answer. The glimmer of delight in her eyes told me I had been played.

"Dora, what's going on?" I wanted an answer, but before she could reply, my attention was pulled back to Mom. I had missed her more than I had realized. "It's good to see you." I stepped forward, ready to embrace her, but the anger in her expression stopped me in my tracks.

Her usual alabaster skin had the color of parchment, bordering on gray, stretched across her fragile frame. The sharp edges of her cheekbones jutted out, and her eyes were rimmed with purple shadows. The years had aged her almost beyond recognition, with her thin arm deprived of all nourishment hanging frail beside her.

"Dora, answer me. Why is she here?" Mom asked between clenched teeth. Her thin hands trembled against her hips.

Pandora's arms snaked around my waist. "She's a sight for sore eyes, isn't she?" She planted a wet kiss on my cheek. "I've missed her. Haven't you?"

I suppressed a shudder, sliding Pandora a guarded look.

"Dora!" Mom cried, throwing her hands in the air. "I told you this couldn't happen. He has a chance to return now. Do you see what this does to our entire family? To Mimi? All of that work, for nothing. How did you even find her?"

"I have the internet, Mom." Pandora rolled her eyes and mimicked Mom throwing her hands in the air. "Ryker might have been from the Stone Age, but we have always had a way to communicate outside of this hellhole."

What had I stepped into? Fear snaked through my veins. I inched backward toward the door.

"Outside communication is limited, and finding someone on the other side is nearly impossible. Trust me, I tried, just so we could avoid this moment. You're lying, Dora." Mom turned to look at me with angry tears spilling down her cheeks. "And you... Goddamn it, you shouldn't have come, Paislee."

Tears stung my eyes. I brushed them away quickly, cursing myself internally for not listening to my instinct.

And the quiet man's words from the hotel's parking garage... How had I not comprehended their meaning? It was as if he'd known what I was about to confront.

The light in the meadow had been my way out for good. I was never meant to come back. The memory crashed into me like a punch to the stomach. I gasped a sharp breath in. If that was how I'd left, then how had I returned?

I shook like a leaf as I turned in a circle, taking in the hundreds of art pieces lining the walls and stacked in corners. More memories of this prison tapped against my skull, sending the pieces of my therapy flushing down the toilet. What I had talked through for years with my therapist wouldn't touch what had really happened here.

Ryker owned us, and we had never had a way to escape until that light had appeared in the meadow. Freedom had been a luxury. I had forgotten how expansive the world was outside this toxic bubble. A dreaded sensation of suffocation pressed down on me, and I struggled to draw in a full breath. My pulse raced erratically in my ears, beating like a drum against my skull. I couldn't stay here.

"Look at what you've done," Pandora said, stepping between me and Mom. "Now she's upset. I thought you missed her."

I didn't have to listen to this garbage. I hadn't wanted

to return to the deceit and dark secrets. If they didn't want me here, I would gladly return to my mundane life, where I had friends and coworkers who treated me better than my own family. I pivoted on my heel and stormed from the room, scooping up my bag outside the door.

"Wait, Paislee," Mom's frantic voice called after me.

I held up my middle finger above my head and kept going. I made it down the hallway in record time. As I turned the corner to the staircase, a hand grabbed my arm. My sharp inhale whistled between my teeth as I yanked my arm out of its grasp.

"Paislee, is it really you?" Mimi asked. Her eyes brightened with joy.

And something else. Fear, maybe. Or trepidation.

She pulled me into her arms. "My baby girl, why have you returned?"

"You too?" I squirmed under her firm hold on me. "I'm leaving. Don't worry."

"You can't leave." She sighed, patting my back and then letting me go. "Let's take your belongings to your room, and we can talk in private." She glanced over her shoulder at the shouting coming from Mom's art room.

"Why the rude greeting?" I nibbled on my bottom lip as I hoisted my bag onto my shoulder, frustration edging its way into irritation.

"You left without a word almost ten years ago, Pais. We've been unable to contact you but knew you were safe, thanks to a friend." Mimi's youthful hand folded over my free arm, and she tugged me in the direction of my old room. "Then you show up out of the blue? You escaped. Why would you return?"

"I couldn't return when I first left." A slow fog of confusion settled in my mind, and the closer we grew to my room, the more difficult it became to understand why or how I'd gotten here. "In fact, I don't know how I made it back today. The entire ten years away is starting to blur, and my memories of here are returning."

She patted my arm with a curt nod. "My point exactly. You shouldn't have come home."

"But Pandora said Ryker was gone, and I had nothing to fear anymore. I wanted to see you, Mimi. She said this might be my last chance to say good-bye." I stopped at the closed door of my room and turned to look at her. "But you don't look ill." I tilted my head and studied her taller frame. Her usual stature remained lean and proud, without a smidgen of frailty showing.

It did not escape my attention that Mimi looked impeccable while Mom appeared to be rapidly aging. The comparison had warning bells ringing in my mind.

"I'm not. I'm as healthy as a horse." She swung open

my bedroom door and stepped inside. "Your sister lied to you. And how did she contact you when no one else could?"

I stared after her as comprehension to her words unraveled inside my mind. Pandora had never lied to me before. I scoffed at my trusting nature. Why would she lie to me?

Mimi waved me inside the room when I didn't budge. "A lot has changed in these ten years. Do you even remember how life was before you left? Do you know what it took for you to escape? How you did it?"

"I remember running from something or someone and then a light in the meadow." A deep rage built in my gut, and I shook my head, unable to pry my thoughts away from the lie. Pandora had tricked me into returning. "I wanted Pandora to come with me, but I couldn't come back. I was all alone in a world unrecognizable to me, and I had to survive without revealing my demon."

Sorrow filled Mimi's eyes. She shifted uncomfortably from one foot to the other. "I'm sorry, baby girl. But even with that hardship, you were better off there."

I knew she spoke the truth, but if Ryker stayed out of the picture, there wasn't anything to fear anymore. Why lie to bring me back?

I absentmindedly walked around my childhood room

and studied the paintings I had picked out as a child. They depicted freedom, with ocean views or rushing waterfalls. Nothing had changed since I'd left. I skimmed my fingers along the wood furniture and sitting chairs, then rubbed my fingertips together and noticed the absence of dust.

My four-poster bed frame remained on the south end wall, my purple curtains pulled open, revealing my old purple-black-and-turquoise bedspread. Several stuffed animals rested against the pillows. I picked up the elephant and held it to my face with a smile warming my heart.

Ryker hadn't been as awful to me or Pandora as he had been to Mom and Mimi. I had trusted him to be good to me, and he usually had been, but the endless trainings and the demon fighting and an underlying resentment had stirred up an energy that had me on high alert. Something warned me that one day he would turn on me and Pandora the way he had Mom and Mimi.

"Why would she lie to me?" I peeled my gaze away from the bed and turned it toward Mimi.

Mimi circled me, running her fingers across my arm. "You're not listening, sweetie. The lie is done and over. The why is irrelevant. We have to find a way for you to leave again." She squeezed my arm and left the room. "Clean up and meet downstairs for dinner. I have some

23

work to do, but we will talk when I have found a solution."

Then she disappeared through the doorway. No explanation. No clarification. Nothing.

Loneliness quickly seeped into my bones. I blew out a breath as I sank to the floor, letting my bag fall to the side with a thud. Ten years by myself I spent fending for myself and surviving on my own, but ten minutes back home and I felt like a useless mess all over again.

FOUR

Pandora

I had avoided Paislee all night, even skipping dinner, despite Mimi's threat to drag me out by my hair. Empty threats—she was all bark and no bite.

But by the time I stirred before seven in the morning, my stomach had other plans. Hunger was gnawing at me, pulling me out of bed and toward the kitchen, where the staff bustled about, arranging breakfast.

Ryker enjoyed a lavish lifestyle and preferred to be catered to, so he arranged for a staff to manage his estate. Most lived in the unreachable human town that lay just beyond the property line. They minded their business, which was Ryker's one hard rule. In exchange, they were paid well and performed their duties excellently.

The rich aroma of coffee filled the air, but I made a beeline for the croissants and snatched one up without hesitation. The first bite melted on my tongue, buttery and sweet, drawing a satisfied moan from my lips.

Cassie, the head cook, shot me an annoyed glance but wisely said nothing, returning to her work. She knew better than to engage. After years of being trapped in this suffocating estate, my resentment for my family—and Ryker—had only sharpened. That alone fueled me to complete what I had started.

Paislee had had ten years of freedom. Now, it was my turn.

I spread cream cheese and jam over a bagel, filled my coffee to the rim, and tiptoed into the dining room. A sliver of morning sunlight slipped across the room. I set my food and drink down and yanked open the heavy curtains, flooding the room with golden light. The rising sun made me smile.

Maybe I despised everyone right now, but I was damn sure going to do it with a smile on my face.

Once my hunger was satisfied, energy surged through me. I bounced through the house, flinging open curtains and belting out an off-key tune just to disrupt the peaceful morning. The thought of rousing the sleeping filled me with wicked delight. The next step to my plan had to unfold today, and Paislee's rage needed to be revealed.

A sharp knock at the front door made me pause. My ears perked up in surprise. Too early for visitors.

I laughed and kept singing, skipping past Arnold, the

26

butler, to reach the door before he could.

I flung it open. Jersey stood on the other side. His brows lifted with suspicious curiosity.

"Are you trying to wake the entire town with that screeching?" he asked with a lopsided smile.

"Jersey!" I threw my arms around his robust frame and squeezed him. "Where have you been hiding yourself?"

He patted my back and quickly stepped away. "I had international business to attend to and returned a few days ago. Thought I would check in with my favorite ladies after some disturbances in town had us on high alert yesterday."

To think, our friendship had begun twelve years earlier, when he'd arrived as a staff member and made fun of Paislee's morning hen hair on day one. We'd laughed so hard, my sides had nearly split. Now, here he was—grown up, with striking green eyes and a wave of chestnut hair that would surely make Paislee swoon.

A pang of jealousy slashed at my insides. His teasing had always been for Paislee, as he only had eyes for her. I shoved away the thought and focused on my plan. I had to see it to the end, and his arrival opened up a perfect opportunity to move it along faster.

"Come in, handsome." I grabbed his hand and pulled him inside. "You have perfect timing. Guess who graced us with her presence?"

"Who?" he asked with a slow smile brightening his eyes.

He had no idea how malicious I had become.

"Your favorite lady in the world." I pointed at the car in the driveway. "Look at that hideous thing. For all the money in the world, I wouldn't be caught dead in that, but she thrived for some reason."

"I don't understand." The two lines between his brows deepened as his smile melted into a frown. "Who is here besides the staff?"

I clicked my tongue at him. "You know who. Exactly the person you have missed for ten years now."

His gaze darted to the car and back to me, then recognition dawned on his face. His expression sharpened enough to cut steel. He grabbed my arm. "She wasn't supposed to come back, Dora. Why is she here?"

"Because I missed her." I playfully slapped his arm and pulled mine out of his grasp. "Didn't you miss her?"

"I've seen her." He blew out a long, shaky breath and turned a venomous glare toward me. "She was finally finding some peace."

My heart dropped. "Were you stalking her?"

He pinched the bridge of his nose and looked heavenward. "No, weirdo. What the hell?"

28

I slammed the door shut and leaned against it. "Why didn't you warn her not to return?"

He dropped his arm and let out a long breath. "I couldn't speak to her. Our realities were split, but when I sensed the divide was thin, I would check in on her." He raked his hand through his dark-brown curls and glanced up the staircase. "Malefi deserved to know her daughter was safe."

I scrunched my face as more animosity swirled in my gut. "My mother knew? Shame on you for never telling me as well. She's my twin. I deserved to know too."

His eyes narrowed to slits. "You seemed glad she left. I didn't realize you wanted to know."

Only because she stole all your and Ryker's attention. Even though her leaving hadn't changed anything... They both continued to obsess over her.

I gave him a dismissive wave of my hand. "She's back. That's all that matters." I pranced away from him, determined to not let his betrayal pull me back down to despair. It wasn't like he'd ever reacted to my advances, and I had long since stopped chasing him. "Come have coffee with me. Maybe she will join us soon, and you can actually speak to her instead of spying on her."

I ignored his loud sigh and smiled at myself when I heard him follow me.

"You know what?" I spun around and nearly ran into him.

He startled and backed up a few steps. "What?"

"Let's go find her now. She will be delighted to see you again." I laughed as a thought came to me. "I can't believe you could have visited her, and you chose to stay in the shadows." I knew he'd done it for Mom, but one last jab wouldn't hurt.

He shook his head and backed farther away from me. "It's early, Dora. She's probably sleeping. And no, you don't understand. The human realities are not easy to break into. The one she entered blocked me from reaching her. I was like a ghost to her."

I understood better than he realized, but I wasn't in the mood to argue. "Nah, she will love to see you again." I sprang forward and grabbed his hand again, then yanked him toward the staircase. "What better way to welcome her home than a visit from our closest childhood friend?"

He dug his heels in, and it stopped me in my tracks.

"Come on, Dora. She will come down when she's ready." A pained expression settled in his eyes.

"You miss her. I can see it. I promise, seeing you again will be the highlight of her day." I was desperate to finish this, and I needed Paislee angry enough to transform. I let his hand drop and walked to the bottom of the stairs, then looked back at him. "If she's sleeping, we will leave her alone."

His silence stretched for several breaths, but then he nodded with uncertainty. "Okay."

He followed me up the stairs and down the corridors to Paislee's door. I knocked.

"Who is it?" Paislee asked.

"Your favorite twin," I replied with a wink at Jersey.

He exhaled through his nose, sharp and forceful as the door flung open.

"I have a bone to—" She stopped short when her gaze landed on Jersey. Her bedhead hair framed her heart-shaped face with puffy eyes from crying. "Jersey! Why are you here?"

Jersey circled me and gathered Paislee into his arms without hesitation, holding her so tight, I wanted to scream. She melted against him as if no time had passed.

"I didn't know you had returned until now. I can see this is a bad time, but I hope you know I am here for you if you need to talk," he whispered in her ear, nuzzling his lips in close to her.

My hearing was impeccable, and he knew it. I grimaced, my deep hatred for everyone jackhammering at my skull.

Paislee held onto Jersey for a few seconds, then

wiggled out of his arms and took a few steps backward. Her gaze met mine as an icy look of disdain rose in her eyes. "This isn't a good time, Jersey. I need to speak with my sister alone."

He glanced my way with a look of pity covering his face. "So it appears. You know how to find me if I am needed." He walked away and rounded the corner without another word.

I gritted my teeth as I watched him leave, then turned my fake smile toward Paislee. She stepped inside, tapping her foot in a rapid, staccato rhythm against the floor. She waved for me to enter her room.

FIVE

Paislee

"You lied!" I screamed at Pandora.

Her eyes darkened. "But I stayed, Paislee. I didn't abandon my family and disappear into thin air. I was here, and I did everything I could to protect Mom and Mimi." She spoke like a dam holding back a flood, every word reinforcing control. "Don't you fucking judge me for falling on the sword while you lived your best life."

"A martyr?" I laughed venomously. "Is that what you want to be? A hero who fell on Ryker's sword? How lame can you be? You didn't protect Mom and Mimi. You handed them to the wolf and looked the other way while he manipulated and tortured them."

"I kept them safe. It was me he focused on after you left, and I did everything to keep his attention directed at me. He would have ripped us apart because of your escape. This is your fault, not mine." She perched herself on the window ledge and peered outside. "You have no idea the sacrifice it took to keep him from coming after you."

I unclenched my fists and rubbed at the fingernail marks in my palms. "Are you saying you did something to Ryker? Is that why he abandoned his estate and gave Mom the run of the place?"

"I'm not saying anything," she spat through gritted teeth. "I don't owe you an explanation, not after you abandoned me to rot with our captor."

I didn't want to fight with her. It felt like a knife to the heart to know she lied, but I had left without a word to her. "You could have come with me. If you had only stopped chasing the fight and giving my location to Ryker's men..." The lie tasted like acid on my tongue, sliding from my lips before I could stop myself. I was no better than her. There had never been a chance for Pandora to follow me through that light, and we both knew it.

I settled onto the edge of my bed, guilt consuming me. Maybe my lies to myself and my actions were the reason we were here in the first place. I had done more damage than I had wanted to admit. It had been easier to keep running and hiding, finding a new life and forgetting about this one.

But they hadn't missed me anyway. If they had, they would have come for me.

"How? The men who saw you walk through that light

could never find it again. And regardless, if I had left Mimi and Mom, then what? They would have been crucified." Pandora gnashed her teeth together, frustration reddening her cheeks. "Someone had to be Ryker's punching bag."

I stared at her, searching for the right words. His punching bag? What did—

A loud knock against the nearby wall jolted me, sending a shiver down my spine. Whispers from the corner had me spinning around on my bed, my heart pounding. My gaze darted around as I searched for an explanation, but besides the two of us, no one else was there. Yet I could have sworn the sound had come from inside the room.

"What's wrong?" Pandora asked, picking her nails as if she were suddenly bored.

My eyebrows knit together in a tangled mess of confusion. "A knock at the door, maybe. Someone whispering. I don't know."

"I didn't hear anything." Pandora rose to her feet and sauntered toward the door. "You really shouldn't allow the ghosts of your past continue to taunt you."

A tall, shadowy figure appeared out of nowhere, shifting into view next to the bed. It swept behind Pandora, slipping toward the outside wall. I leaped up and took a sudden step back, opening and closing my mouth but unable to form the words I wanted to scream. The figure whirled to face me, freezing as I stared wide-eyed at it. Time stood still for several breaths and then it inched toward me.

An icy chill traveled down my spine.

"What's your problem?" Pandora turned back toward me, throwing me a frosty look.

I snapped my fingers and pointed, bouncing on my toes. "Dora, don't you see it?"

The figure came to a sudden halt, and a foggy mist blew around it like a soft wind had swept through the room.

Pandora snorted. "Good grief, Paislee. Get a grip. You've always been the dramatic one."

"Wait. What?" I glowered at her, momentarily forgetting about the ghost. "I've never been the dramatic one. That's a whole lot of projection vomit you have going on."

The shadowy figure leaned in closer, quickly drawing my attention back to it. Its long, pointed nose and dark eyes came into focus. It blinked.

Oh. My. God. A wave of terror gripped me as I staggered backward, barely suppressing a scream. A real ghost was haunting me. It darted closer, even when I tried to leap out of its path, and came within inches of colliding with me. At the last moment, it swooshed past, vanishing through the nearest wall.

Terror twisted through me like a cold wind, leaving me unsteady and breathless.

"My point exactly. The dramatic one."

Pandora's laughter startled me back to reality just as she left the room, slamming the door behind her.

I stared at the closed door, drawing in sharp breaths to calm my pounding heart and trying to find my focus. After several silent moments, I turned my attention to the wall the shadow had slipped through, wondering if my mind was playing tricks on me. My fingers trembled as I rubbed my clammy palms together and walked closer to the wall. There was nothing out of the ordinary to explain what I had seen.

I should never have returned, and I would rectify that mistake now.

My bag lay open near the bathroom door. Several items were strewn over the nearby chair, and my electronics were piled in the corner. I scooped them up and shoved them into my bag, then hauled it to my bed. I organized everything inside to fit the rest of my belongings.

A cold breeze blew behind me, and I dropped my

phone charger onto the bedspread. I slowly turned, examining the room inch by inch. The curtains remained unmoved, and the door was still shut, but the chill in the room had dropped the temperature by several degrees.

I wrapped my arms around my chest as I walked the perimeter, testing each lock on the windows. I ran my hands along the walls, looking for a gap or cracks, but after circling the room, I found nothing.

But every muscle in my body screamed that I was being watched. The cold crept along my skin, sending goose bumps traveling down my arms and legs. I spun in a circle, and as my gaze darted past the corner where my electronics had lain, the tall, dark figure shifted into view.

My heart leaped into my throat. I spun toward the door, tripping over my feet as I tried to run. My ankle twisted, and I fell face-first onto the carpet. Terror crashed through me, nearly paralyzing me against the carpet, but somehow I rolled to my back and wormed away from the figure. I squealed as it swept closer, then it stopped abruptly, leaning over me until it was inches from my face.

Its face faded in and out like a steady heartbeat, looming just above me.

A scream wrenched up my throat and burst from my lips, startling the ghost. It fell away from me but froze a few feet away. I scrambled backward. A dark fog billowed in front of me, masking the ghost from my view. My body stiffened with my pulse pounding in my ears. Unable to make sense of the darkness surrounding me, I reached back and touched the foot of the sitting chair, then used it to guide me to my feet.

I heard the thud of my phone and watched it bounce close to the expanding fog. I inched away, never taking my eyes off the darkness. I reached backward and felt along the walls until the door was under my fingertips.

The figure held out a hand. "Don't," a low, whispery voice called from the fog.

I found the doorknob and yanked open the door, then dashed out of the room, refusing to look back as I ran.

SIX

Pandora

I slipped down the stairs and through the kitchen, snagging another croissant as I circled the long island. The kitchen staff were taking most of the food into the dining room, and I heard Mimi's bright and sparkling laugh as she joked with the servers.

We were trapped on these grounds, and Mimi remained happy as a clam. Or was she wearing a mask of make-believe, similar to mine? I wouldn't put it past her. This family was full of secrets and betrayal.

Do you want to trade lives with Paislee? Slip through the same portal?

Ryker's voice lived rent-free in my head. Every day I ran his questions through my mind, reminding myself why I had chosen this path.

The door to the outside was already open, with the remaining house staff arriving for the day. I ignored those who were outside and raced for the underground tunnel doors.

Ryker had hid the entrance to the tunnel doors at the edge of the estate, only showing me when I was ready to bargain with him. But I always knew this was where Mom had banished him, sealing him and his men within the tunnels for eternity.

Magic came with a cost, and she was paying dearly.

I hated those words, and I despised Mom for including me in the curse—binding me to these lands, along with Mimi and herself. All to protect her precious, weak Paislee. It was always about Paislee.

I pushed through the overbrush, gently nudging the branches and twigs out of my way to avoid breaking any in case Mom ever checked on her prisoners. A few feet in, the oversized wooden door loomed in front of me. The dark mahogany wood was the opposite of the rest of the estate's white doors and marked a place no one liked to venture. For good reason. Before Ryker had been banished, I was warned ghosts haunted these tunnels.

A cloud of uncertainty loomed around me as I thought of Paislee's knocking ghost. Maybe the house was haunted as well. Good thing my stay in this godforsaken place was coming to an end.

I twisted the doorknob and shoved it open.

A gust of stale air filled my nose, and I sneezed so loudly, I swore I had woken the dead. But with my luck, it had only stirred Ryker's guards. I reached around the doorframe and flipped the large light switch to the up position, and an orange illumination flooded the tunnel ahead.

My gaze swept over the length of the corridor. Empty. I blew out a slow breath and eased the door shut, leaving it open a crack for a possible quick escape.

"Ryker," I whispered, stepping gingerly down the cobblestone floor. "Where are you, you old bastard?"

"Bastard?" a man said behind me. His chuckle was low and humorless, like he was savoring my pain.

I whirled around and found Ryker leaning against the stone wall with a slow, poisonous smile curving his lips. His blond hair lay swept to one side, with the wisps on the other side tucked behind his ear.

"You know I hate when you sneak up on me!" I snapped, circling him to put myself between him and the door.

When he'd whispered through the grates in the garden, asking me to meet him at the door for the first time, I had found it amusing, especially knowing Mom's spell had failed. But the idea he had planted in my mind had consumed me since that moment. I hated everything about him, but my obsession to see Paislee pay for leaving me and to find freedom for the first time festered just below my skin, to the point of madness.

I had to see this through to the end.

"Have you convinced Paislee to come home?" He drummed his left fingers against his thigh, while idly playing with the hem of his shirt with the other hand.

"Right to business, eh?" I nervously twirled the ends of my hair around my fingers.

His gaze flickered to mine. "Is there any other reason for us to converse? You want to leave the boundaries of my estate, and I want to walk among the living again. What else is there to discuss?"

He faded slightly, reminding me that his ethereal self was what stood before me and his physical form remained stuck. He couldn't touch me, even if he tried. But that didn't settle my heart from hammering against my chest.

"Fine. Paislee arrived home yesterday. Everything is in motion. Where do I complete the ritual, and once it is done, how do I know you will hold up your end of the bargain?" I settled my hands on my hips and stood up straighter, doing my best to appear confident despite my racing pulse.

His smile brightened, and he pushed away from the wall. "I knew you could do it, Dora. You are the smart one. That's why you are who you are."

"You mock me, Ryker." I inched closer to the door, not

43

wanting him anywhere near me. "You have never believed I'm smart, and you couldn't care less who I am. If you gave a damn about me, you would have allowed me to be free like my sister."

He laughed and slow-clapped in my direction. "You have me there. But I do think you are the smarter one. Whether that would classify you as intelligent is beside the point."

"Get on with it!" I hissed between clenched teeth. My loathing for him intensified each passing second.

His arms fell to his sides. "Take the items you have gathered to the center garden, along with the vials of blood from each one of you. Recite the chants *exactly* as I taught you, and follow the instructions to the letter. With all four of you within the boundaries of the estate, the rest will come together smoothly."

My annoyance flared, right alongside my growing rage. "And what is with the vials of blood? I just drop the blood in the garden and poof, it's done?"

"Don't drop them, smarty-pants." He rolled his eyes at my questions, dismissing them with a mocking wave.

If it weren't for his incorporeal state of being, I would have jabbed my fingers into those blue, condescending eyes. And then twisted those fuckers right out of their sockets.

"Slowly sprinkle every last drop of blood through the grate as you recite the spell. Do not skip one step. And, Pandora?"

"What?" I barked, swallowing down the ball of fury rising in my throat.

A smirk rose on his lips. "If you attempt to leave before I am free, you will only find yourself back in the estate with less space to roam."

I gave him a mock salute. "Noted." I gripped the edge of the door and heaved it open. "Anything else?"

"Do it today, Dora." He jabbed his thumb over his shoulder. "I've grown impatient, and so have they."

One of his guards slipped into view and drew his finger across his throat with a pointed look at me. I caught the threat, which only enraged me further. I hated living like this, and I couldn't help but antagonize the men like they had done to me through my childhood.

I pulled open the door farther, white-knuckling the doorknob. "I'll do it when I'm good and ready. Learn some patience, Ryker." I slipped through the doorway as several more of his men rounded the corner.

"Dragging your feet will only lead to more pain," Ryker called after me.

I bristled from his meaning, knowing he would follow through with it. I yanked the door shut without a reply.

45

My fingers shook as I clasped my hands together, hating myself for what I was about to do.

SEVEN

Paislee

I found myself on the stairs, trembling like a leaf with my knees gathered against my chest, when I finally came to my senses. My fingernails clawed into the stair railing as I heaved in one breath after another, doing my best to convince my mind to chill the fuck out.

Had I been hallucinating? This estate was filled with nightmares, but never the ghostly ones.

Ryker's bellowing voice had terrified me as a child. His rage-filled expression when he stood over me, threatening to punish Mom or Mimi if I didn't comply, had been enough motivation to obey. And his eerie and quiet men, who walked and guarded the home and grounds, frightened me with their obscene, bulging muscles and hardened expressions. As a child, I would have done anything to avoid them.

But none of it compared to seeing someone or something mostly invisible invading my childhood room. I didn't know what kind of fresh hell had been allowed in this estate, but I didn't know if the better choice was it or Ryker. That man had been a lot of things, but he'd never come into my room without permission.

After my heart rate steadied and I regained my focus, I studied the stairs and the main floor below me. The spiral staircase had been my and Pandora's favorite part of the house—a dream for any girl to walk down as a princess. But we weren't royalty, just captives of a controlling man who wanted their mother more than anyone in this world. He would burn down our world to keep her tame and under his control.

His obsession never made sense to me, but asking questions only led to weeks of punishment that included scrubbing tile with a toothbrush while under the watchful eye of Ryker's men. The memory made me cringe. It had been easier to pretend we lived in a fairy tale and could escape to the forest whenever possible.

I made my way down the stairs, inspecting the bright entryway and the tall beams that doubled as bookcases. The artwork and priceless literature on each shelf were one of a kind and had been handpicked by Ryker. The man had been a tyrant, but a cultured one at that.

I stopped in the dining room and found no one there, but plenty of breakfast food and drinks for my picking had been laid out on the table.

I did miss this.

The ghost hadn't followed me, and with the kitchen staff hustling in the next room, I felt somewhat safe to indulge in breakfast. I wrapped my arms around my torso and walked the length of the room, checking every corner until I was satisfied.

The pancakes were cold, but the syrup had been warmed. I slathered the cakes with butter, then drowned them in maple syrup. After two cups of coffee and a full belly, I laced up my boots, threw on my jacket, and set out for the forest.

If I was going to leave again, I needed to say a proper good-bye to my childhood. I didn't have the chance the last time.

The dry leaves crunched beneath my boots as the crisp air curled around me, ushering me into the shadows beneath the trees' canopy. This I missed—the hush of the forest, the eerie sounds that would send most people running. But normal had never been a trait of my family. I had inherited my demon from Mom, and any creature with a nose knew better than to come too close.

Pandora and I had used the forest as our sanctuary from Ryker. For a reason unknown to us, he feared the darkness of the forest and forbade us to enter without his men accompanying us. But we had always found a way to slip away from them and spend our afternoons in the trees.

I stopped where the sun barely breached the ground, and darkness folded gently over me. The comfort reminded me of my sister and the safety the trees had provided. I tilted my head upward and drew in a long breath, remembering how we had played.

Once upon a time, we had been inseparable.

"You and I were supposed to be the same." Pandora *swung from the branches of the trees. "Don't you get it, Pais? We weren't supposed to be different in any way. Ravens fly in pairs, not all alone."*

I settled onto one of the larger branches and leaned against the trunk. "We can't be the exact same on everything, Dora. Don't you want something to call your own?"

"No. We belong together and should be the same." She *flipped to the ground and landed on her feet. "It's unfair anyway. Why am I the smaller one?"*

I hadn't had an answer for her. Her dark curls had bounced out of sight after we'd stared at one another in silence for several minutes. I'd stayed quiet, and she ran. Those were our coping skills.

Maybe it was unfair. But life was unfair.

In the end, even though Pandora had mastered it better, I had been the one to run the farthest. Now, I was paying the price for my decision.

"Paislee, is that you?" a male voice called from the shadows.

I stiffened, clenching my fists to my sides. The ghostly face I had seen in my room haunted my memory, and fear gripped my chest at the thought of him invading my privacy once again. My gaze darted toward the voice.

A familiar figure stepped closer, and I blew out a laugh. I smiled at Jersey.

"Can't scare you away for long, can I?" I started walking again, brushing past him.

"You have never scared me." He fell into step next to me. "Your sister, on the other hand, she's another story."

"She's always been another story. I don't miss her manipulations, but I did miss her." I slipped my arm through his and pulled him against my side, dodging the small twigs bouncing from the wind. "How have you been? Did you miss me?"

"Yes. Every day." He reached over and brushed my hair out of my face. "I wish I could have gone with you."

I kicked a pebble. "I didn't have a choice. It all happened so quickly, and it was either lose my opportunity or move forward, never looking back."

I stole a glance at his face, noting the dark shadow on his chin, something he hadn't had in our teenage years.

The scruff suited him, adding a touch of distinction that complemented his green eyes and brown hair.

"You know it nearly broke your mother to have you gone?" He pulled me to a stop and gathered both my hands within his. "It was heart-wrenching to find out. No good-byes. Just poof, you were gone."

I felt old wounds reopening, frustration boiling up like an untamed tide. "Everyone is acting as if I planned this. Why do I have to continue to explain myself as if none of you took the time to find me?" I pulled my hands free. "My mother never came looking for me, and my letters went unanswered every year."

He closed his eyes for a few seconds, then refocused on me. "I'm sorry. It's more complicated than I'm making it out to be, and I know better than anyone that you didn't mean to leave us behind." He exhaled, slow and careful, as if letting out too much might scare me away. "I missed you more than words can express, and I'm doing a horrible job of telling you."

"We were young." I averted my gaze downward, to stare at the ground between us, and released an exaggerated breath. "I have never stopped loving you, but once I was out in the real world, I couldn't talk myself into returning. I needed space from my family and especially Ryker. The freedom..." I sighed again, remembering the relief. "I could be anyone I wanted out there, and no one would be the wiser."

His fingers grazed my lips. "I do understand why you didn't return."

"Do you?" I melted from his touch, but too much time had passed. Rekindling what we had back then seemed too big, especially when I had no intention of staying.

He cupped my chin and tilted my face upward. "Pandora always believed you and her were meant to be together forever. Maybe that's true, but maybe you belong with me."

"Maybe I don't belong with anyone." I grabbed his wrist and pulled his hand away. "I'm not here to pick up where we left off. You do understand that, don't you?"

Hurt flashed in his eyes, but he quickly blinked it away and held up his hands. "You're right. I'm pushing boundaries I had no intention of pushing. I'm sorry I keep putting my foot in my mouth. Can I start over?"

I shifted from one to the other and waved a dismissive hand at his guarded stance. "I'm just surprised, Jersey. This entire charade has caught me off guard. Pandora. Her lies. My mom and her fading health. You." I waved my hand again at him. "I feel like I've hopped from one dream to the next."

He dropped his arms to his sides and stepped in close

again. "I don't want to be on your list. I want to be the one you can be sure about. Paislee?"

I took a step back, pressing my back against a tree trunk. "Yes?"

He came in closer and leaned in, studying every inch of my face. "I have so much to tell you." He kissed my forehead. "But first, can I tell you I still love you?

"I don't know, can you?" I wanted to reach out, to run my fingers down his scruffy chin, but hesitation gripped me.

His gaze flickered to my lips for a second, before he quickly looked away. The space between them narrowed. "After all this time, nothing has changed. I never stopped loving you."

"No girlfriend? Wife?" I asked, tilting my head, waiting. Not pushing, just waiting.

He shook his head, placing his arm on the trunk above my head and leaning in even closer. "I tried to move on. Trust me. There was nothing easy about losing you. Moving on would have made it bearable."

His intense gaze locked with mine, and a sudden energetic charge ignited between us. My breath hitched in my throat. Jersey's face faded, and the memories of his touch sprang to the surface as if they had been held under water, drowning for years. The air warmed around me.

My life before I left Ryker's property played through my mind like a movie. I had forgotten so much.

But how?

Jersey lightly touched my forearm. "Are you okay?"

I gave him a quick nod as I refocused on our conversation. "So why didn't you?" I worried my lower lip as a spark of desire flared to life deep within me. I hadn't meant to let him fade from my memory, but time had stolen him away. The ache for his touch crashed over me, raw and undeniable.

"No one held my attention long enough." He shrugged, fidgeting with something in his pocket. "My life became more complicated, and distractions weren't my thing."

I trailed my fingers along the back of his wrist, then pulled his hand out of his pocket. "What if I distracted you now?"

A smile tugged at his lips, and he circled his free arm around my waist. "You could never be a distraction. You are exactly who I want to be focused on."

I traced my fingers down his cheek, across his chest, and circling down to his abdomen, never taking my gaze off his face. Those green eyes drew me in like a magnet, as if no time had passed, and when he moved closer, I didn't resist. His lips pressed softly to mine, flooding my mind with our teenage years and our undeniable connection.

His fingers tightened around the back of my neck, and he drew me closer with one quick move. He wrapped his arms around me and deepened the kiss with his tongue, exploring my lips and mouth. Heat curled down my spine and I leaned into him, relishing the euphoria.

A twig snapped nearby, and we both froze. Jersey broke apart our kiss and leaned backward, peering over my shoulder. His eyes crinkled with amusement, and he pointed.

"Look." His hands curled over my shoulders, and he turned me around.

A herd of deer slipped through the brush, paying us no attention as they circled the tree we were standing next to. The scene sent a spark through me, igniting a wildfire of delight. I had forgotten how magical my childhood had been in this forest. It may have been hell on Earth at the estate, but this... This I missed dearly.

The thought of the estate reminded me of why I had come to the forest. A hum of unease returned to my mind.

"There was someone in my room today." I glanced at Jersey. "Someone or something I could barely see. But I'm not crazy, Jersey. I saw them, and they were watching me. What has happened to this place? I feel like there is a storm brewing, but I'm not sure where or when it will hit."

He scratched his nose, and two lines appeared between his brows. "I don't know all the details of what has happened while you have been away, but I do know there are ghosts on this property."

"Ghosts?" I shook my head, watching the last deer walk past us "I lived here for seventeen years, and I never encountered an intangible entity. There might be demons within us but never walking among us."

He laughed. "You make it sound so normal to have a demon. And how do you know they don't walk among us? Maybe you are seeing them now because you did escape and have a different perspective. Maybe they have always been there."

I didn't like the sound of that either. I pressed my palms against my cheeks and walked away from him, kicking at the leaves and twigs.

"I've got to leave again. There's no point in beating around the bush. I don't care if this place is or was or always has been haunted." I stopped and threw him a look over my shoulder.

"I don't think it will be that easy." He took a step toward me.

I held out my hand to stop him, heat rising in my cheeks. "Don't, Jersey. I can't stay. This place had me on the verge of suicide before, and today was only a reminder as to why I was so desperate to escape. Whatever is hiding in the shadows is no better than what had been right in front of my face as a child."

"You need to speak to your mother," he whispered, sadness clouding his features. "I can't give you the answers, Pais. I love you, and I know your mom adores you. Please speak with her before you make any decisions."

"I'm not staying," I snapped. A sharp heat burned between my ribs, frustration and guilt tangling together. "It doesn't matter what she says."

He closed the distance between us but stopped a few inches away. "I'm not asking you to stay. I'm asking you to listen. It's important, Paislee," he said with rushed, breathless sentences, as if he were afraid to be cut off. "We are more than what you have been told."

"We?" He had never been one of us. He was my dearest friend and former lover, but not a demon like my family.

He gathered my hands in his and kissed my knuckles. "I'll return soon. Speak to your mother. Maybe the ghost in your room is something better than what was in your past. Maybe running this time will not be the answer. And maybe, just maybe, the truth will finally provide you with a reason to break the spell over your family."

I staggered back a step, shocked by his words. He pulled me back toward him and pressed his lips against my forehead, then jogged away, leaving me with more questions than I had before he had arrived.

EIGHT

Pandora

A branch smacked me in the face when I turned away from the tunnel door.

I rubbed my cheek and grimaced at the smaller trees. "It's not what you think. This will be the best for everyone." Definitely best for me.

I pushed forward and made it past the branches and brush without another incident, but I felt the energy intensify around me. The trees knew something was off. Once they realized my betrayal, I didn't know if I would ever be forgiven.

I was rounding the corner toward the estate when a figure moved in my peripheral vision. Fear twisted in my stomach, and my pulse quickened from an unspoken tension. Mimi stepped onto the path directly in front of me.

Her brows furrowed, one arching slightly higher than the other, as her eyes narrowed with a flicker of uncertainty. "Were you in the tunnels? Do you know what your mother would do if she found out you entered them?"

My mouth twisted into a scowl. "Then don't tell her." I stormed forward, knocking shoulders with her when I passed her.

Mimi let out a long, frustrated groan and muttered under her breath.

Irritation bit at the back of my skull. My grandmother was thriving in this pitiful prison, while I suffered. I had to find a way out of here once and for all, and I would burn it all down before I would let anyone stop me.

I whirled around to confront Mimi and almost ran into her. She stopped short, and her foot tapped against the ground with an uneven, irritated rhythm.

"What were you doing in the tunnels?"

My mouth twitched to bite back a sharp retort. I sucked in a sharp breath through my nose. "Let's talk in private."

"Yes, let's." Mimi patted my arm and walked around me. "Come to my suite."

"Right behind you," I replied, following several feet behind her.

Her long, silver hair hung to her waist, curling halfway down in spirals. I admired her strength, and even when she was mad, she held herself high like a queen. When Paislee had gone missing, Mimi had been the one to remain calm and collected while Mom and Ryker had panicked. I had watched, grief-stricken and confused, but then sided with Mimi to stop the search for Paislee. My trust in Mimi had been solid.

Geez, did I regret that decision.

The cryptic answers following their decision that day had infuriated me.

It's for your own safety, Mimi had told me.

Fuck safety. I wanted freedom so badly, I could taste it.

"Mimi?"

She slowed her walk and looked over her shoulder at me. "Yes, Dora?"

I caught up to her and matched her steps. "Why didn't you want us to find Paislee? Maybe I could have found a way to leave as well. You didn't need me here to entrap Ryker."

"Because you were reckless." She stopped in her tracks and turned to face me, palming my cheeks with both hands. "Paislee's caution would keep her safe. You?" Her breath hitched in her throat as if the thought disturbed her. "I couldn't see a future where you would survive, and it terrified me."

My hands balled into fists at my side, nails digging into my palms. I pulled away from her. "Your visions have always been worthless. That's a horrible reason for not allowing me my freedom."

Hurt flashed across Mimi's face, but she quickly steeled her expression and shrugged. "Was it?" She continued toward the main house at a quick pace.

I jogged to catch up with her. "Yes! It was. Paislee was always your favorite. That's what this has come down to. Her demon makes you proud. Just like Mom's does."

"Jealousy looks ugly on you." She kept her gaze forward.

Her words stung. A storm of angry thoughts churned in my mind, each one sharper than the last.

"Paislee's escape wasn't easy to see in advance," Mimi muttered, breaking the silence after a few minutes. "If I had known before you entered the forest that day…"

Her pause stretched on as we made our way to the back staircase.

I stopped at the base of the stairs. "What? If you had known what?"

She shook her head and continued the climb. "It doesn't matter. What is done is done."

I gripped the stair rail, my knuckles turning white with the pressure. And this was exactly why I couldn't stay here.

We walked the rest of the way to Mimi's suite in

silence. After closing the door, I turned to face the woman I both adored and despised the most in the world. My existence was never good enough for her, no matter what I had done to please her.

"We are alone now. Why were you in the tunnels?" Mimi asked, pouring herself a glass of cucumber water.

"To make sure Ryker hadn't escaped." I grabbed one of the glasses from her kitchenette shelves and poured seltzer water into it. "With Paislee here, I wasn't sure how it would affect the hold on him."

"You're lying to me. How did you find out that was where your Mom had imprisoned Ryker?" Mimi peered at me over the rim of her glass before taking a drink.

I bristled from the accusation, even though it was true. "Why did you ask if you weren't going to believe me?"

She ran her finger around the rim of her glass. "I had hoped for the truth."

I threw my empty hand into the air. "What do you want from me? For me to have never been born? To leave you three to live as a happy family? What is it with you and this animosity?"

Mimi's expression softened. "There isn't any animosity, my love. Never has been. But I know you, and after you tricked Paislee to return home, I know you are up to something, even with the block your Mom's spell has put on my visions. What is it?"

I swallowed a mouthful of water and shook my head. "I told you. I wanted to know we are safe. She might not be able to leave again, but at least we can be a family without Ryker's tyranny hanging over us."

Mimi studied me for several breaths before sighing. "Your eyes tell me you are lying, Dora. If you cannot speak the truth, then maybe we should involve your mother after all." She set down her glass and reached for her phone.

"No!" I hollered. I rushed forward and yanked the phone from her hands, then tossed it across the room.

It thudded against the wall and tumbled to the ground.

"Dora!" Mimi stormed past me, heading toward her phone.

"I'm sorry, Mimi. I have no other choice." I tapped each of her shoulders. "The bind is complete. The containment will hold. None will venture near. None will hear your cries. Twenty-four hours before it wears."

Mimi's eyes widened, her pupils shrinking like a trapped animal. "What have you done?"

I took several steps away from her, scooping up her phone and pocketing it, before putting some distance between us. I scratched the back of my neck and fidgeted with my necklace, inching closer to the door.

The taste of guilt was bitter, clinging to my tongue like tar. I shoved down the feeling, determined to see this through to the end.

"I learned from the best. Don't worry, you have free reign in your suite, and I have left you food in your drawers." I shot her a quick glance to make sure she didn't follow. "Tomorrow this will all be over." I flashed her a peace sign and slipped out of the suite with a soft click of the door shutting.

My hand lingered against the wood door for several breaths as I searched for the strength to carry my plan to the end.

NINE

Paislee

I raced up the stairs when I returned to the estate, taking two at a time. When I made it to Mom's art room, I knocked once, then pushed open the door. A dusty aroma of charcoal mixed with hints of oil paint and turpentine assaulted my senses.

My eyes watered from the smell, and I wiped at them as I stepped inside the room. "Mom?"

The curtains were fully closed, casting dark shadows across the walls. A low light flickered at the far end of the room, where a couch and several chairs surrounded a coffee table with a half-completed puzzle.

"Here." Mom's hand rose from the couch, and she waved. "Come in, Paislee."

I picked my way through the piles of art supplies. "Can I talk to you? I know you're not happy I'm here, but—"

Mom bolted upright, and the color quickly drained from her cheeks. "I missed you, Pais. I really, really missed you." She hung her head in her hands. "It's not that

I'm not happy you're here. I'm thrilled to see your face again." Her gaze lifted, and tears glistened in her eyes.

"Then why were you angry at Dora for asking me to come home?" I settled onto the arm of the nearest chair.

"Why didn't you call? Or write? Anything?" Mom wiped at her tears. "I couldn't find you, and it broke me. Weakened me."

I saw her for the first time. Really saw her. Her face had thinned, and her cheeks had sunk in, with her skin wrinkling around her eyes and her mouth deeper than Mimi's. The dark circles under her eyes made her appear older than a middle-aged woman. My blood turned cold when I really took in the difference between her and Mimi.

"Mom, are you sick?" I rushed to her side and sat next to her.

"He took a lot from me after you left." She reached up and ran her hand through my hair with a soft smile growing on her lips. "You are so beautiful, Paislee. And kindhearted. You deserved a better family."

I took her hand in mine. "What did he take from you?"

Ryker had told me if I left, he would find me. I'd never imagined he would harm Mom.

"I haven't been able to summon her, Paislee." Her voice shook as she squeezed my hand. "I know you hate yours, but we were gifted these creatures. He clipped my wings, and I will never get them back."

I held in my gasp, then swallowed it hard with a shake of my head. "How? I thought he had been cut off from physically harming you after what happened last time. How could he possibly do that to you?"

"I'm weak now. I've aged faster in the last few years than ever before in my entire existence. Mimi will outlive me." She kissed my cheek, then leaned back against the cushion. "It was bound to happen eventually."

"But how, Mom? And what do I need to do to rectify this?"

"You can't do anything about it. Ryker is not here. There is no way of undoing what has been done, and even if there were, I don't know if I want to be cured." She closed her eyes, exhaling a long breath. "It's too much, Pais. I've lived long enough and experienced too much heartache because of that man. You and Pandora will live free from him, and that is enough for me to die happy."

My gaze traveled around the cluttered room as I looked for anything that would clue me in as to what had happened since I'd left. But nothing stood out to me. Ryker had insisted Mom continue her art and sculptures, praising her for each one as if they were the most beautiful pieces he had ever seen. His relationship with her had been a mystery to me and Pandora, one of intense adoration from him with a mixture of deep hatred that surfaced at the most precarious of moments.

Mom's detached emotions had puzzled us further, but we weren't allowed to ask questions. Malefi and Ryker was an untouchable subject, and even now I sensed resistance from Mom's answers.

I refocused on Mom and patted her knee. "How do you know he won't return?"

She glanced up at me without raising her chin. "He can't return. The only people who know how to bring him back are me and Ryker. And Ryker isn't talking to anyone anymore."

"Mom?" I sighed and grabbed her knee. "What did you do? Is this why you're ill? Did you do something to him?

"Everything I have done has been to protect you." She closed her eyes again and pressed her palms against her lids. "That is why I'm angry with Dora. You were free from this. Free from him. I made sure he would never find you, even if it meant I would never see you again."

My heart skipped a beat. "Mom, no. What did you do?"

"You can't leave, Pais. Ever again. I won't undo the spell, not if it means he will be free again." Her arms fell to her sides, and she twisted her torso to lie on the couch.

"I will die knowing you are safe from him."

The spell on our family... just like Jersey had mentioned. "What do you mean I can't leave?" I shot to my feet.

Her lower lip quivered. "We are stuck here. Forever. The only way to unbind our family from this property is to free that asshole, and it's not going to happen."

"He didn't leave on his own then?" I leaned over Mom and touched her shoulder. "Where is he? I will fix this. Please let me fix this."

She softly sighed and closed her eyes. "You can't, baby. This is our lives now."

"But, Mom, I found a way out before. We never left the estate grounds when I was younger either, until I found that light in the meadow." I clasped my hands together and pressed them against my chin, doing my best to shove away the panic swirling like a hurricane in my stomach. "I don't believe we are trapped, and I will prove it."

She scooted to a seated position again. "What light in the meadow?" Mom's brows furrowed, but a spark of interest blazed in her eyes.

"How do you think I escaped?" I sank to the couch and grabbed her hand. "Did you think I just walked out of here, even with Ryker's control over us?"

She slowly nodded as her eyes glazed over in thought. "That day, Paislee..." A shiver visibly rushed over her. "There was a booming snap that shook the estate and then dark clouds rolled in with lightning striking continuously across the grounds. Pandora arrived home wet and terrified, screaming that you couldn't be found."

I squeezed her hand and then released it. "Because I had gone through the light. Everything was different on the other side."

Her focus snapped back to me. "Different how?"

"You barely existed to me." I pressed my lips together and shot her a sheepish look.

She sat up straight, but the color further drained from her cheeks, leaving her pale as a ghost. "What does that mean?"

"You first, Mom." I patted her knee and then slid a few inches away from her so I could turn and look at her fully. "I want to know everything. No more secrets."

TEN

Pandora

I swung the door open, hitting the doorjamb with a thud. Mom and Paislee sat at the end of the room, bathed in the yellow light from the lamp. I strolled in, scrunching my forehead, when a sharp stab of jealousy sliced through my heart.

"There you are." My gaze drifted from Mom over to Paislee. "Did you tell her? Did you tell her how you entrapped us here to protect her? Your precious, favorite child."

Mom straightened her position despite the pain flashing across her expression. "Don't. You know that's not true."

"I obviously know nothing. I'm the dumb one. Right, Mom?" I sank onto one of the chairs across from them, picking up a pencil from the arm and tossing it into the air.

Paislee leaned toward me. "What happened? Mom isn't telling me everything."

"Of course she's not." I smacked the arm of the chair, then jabbed the pencil in Mom's direction. "She always protected you, and here she thinks she is doing it again."

Mom grumbled something under her breath, raking her hands through her dark hair and tugging at the roots. "Are you here to verbally punch me? You're the one who tricked your sister into returning to a place she can never leave again."

I bristled from the remark, fidgeting with the hem of my shirt as I focused on Paislee. "Do you really want to know the truth? There's no going back after I tell you."

"No," Mom snapped.

"Yes." Paislee shot Mom an icy look, then rose to her feet and paced the floor in front of me. "I'm here. Just give it to me straight."

I flipped the pencil in the air again and caught it. "Suit yourself. The day after you left, Ryker nearly burned down the forest searching for you. His men hacked at dozens of trees and tore them down one by one, trying to clear the way so Ryker could gain access without the trees attacking him. The only reason he stopped is because the trees started ripping his men apart."

"This isn't necessary," Mom said, throwing me a stern look.

"Stop, Mom. I want to know. What did he do?" Paislee

74

wrung her hands together before sinking to the edge of her seat.

I held up my free hand. "Which actually brings up a great point that has never been answered. The forest." I rolled the pencil between my fingers, narrowing my eyes at Mom. "This is Ryker's property, but the trees despise him. Why?"

Mom opened her mouth, then quickly slammed it shut. She shook her head.

"They strengthen us but weaken him. You don't think I pay attention, but I do." I crossed one leg over the other and leaned forward, turning my attention to Paislee. "He wanted us in there but only on his terms. No one can ever tell us why."

The corners of Paislee's lips twitched as her frown deepened. "It really doesn't make sense. I see that, but before we get sidetracked, I want to know what Ryker did."

"For fuck's sake, Paislee. He forced Mom to shift and go into the forest to hunt you." Saying it out loud sounded worse than it had been, but satisfaction from Paislee's surprised expression warmed my heart.

"What?" Paislee sat up straight, her gaze darting between Mom and me. "I wasn't there. His men saw me vanish through the light. Why would he believe he could find me in there?"

I flung the pencil at her. She ducked, and the pencil stuck in the wall behind her.

"Dora!" Mom exclaimed, sliding to the edge of her seat.

"What the fuck." Paislee's voice was low and dangerously controlled. She rubbed her forehead as if the pencil had struck her, but her expression remained calm.

I would have to do better than this.

"I wasn't even aiming it at her." I rolled my eyes at Mom. "Get a grip."

"Finish." Paislee eyed me with a cold, unwavering stare, her pupils constricted like a predator tracking prey.

There she is.

"When she returned without you, he did what he had done years before and forced her to sleep. But as always, we don't get to know how he does that to her." A bitter laugh escaped my lips, and I ignored Mom's hurt expression. This was her fault. "It's like a cruel joke on us all, the never-ending lies they tell us."

"Then what?" Paislee's head tilted slightly to one side, her slow inhale hinting at the questions lingering on her lips.

"I already told you," Mom whispered.

Paislee pinned me with her glare. "Dora?"

I gave her a half shrug. "While she was sleeping, I watched his men cut off her wings."

Paislee's jaw clenched so tightly, it twitched. I shifted nervously and snuck a quick look in Mom's direction. She closed her eyes, sighing in defeat.

Paislee slowly turned to face Mom, smoothing the wrinkles in her pants as she shifted. "He really did it. And you let him?"

"I was asleep," Mom murmured, hanging her head. "Did you think I was lying?"

"I see. No, I thought it was more metaphorical, not actual. Didn't Mimi bind him from forcing sleep on you?" Paislee turned again to face me, every muscle taut with silent fury. "In fact, where was Mimi in all of this?"

"With me. Holding me back. What did you expect her to do? Poke their eyes out? She and I have never been the stronger of the four of us, and any power Mimi had over Ryker had been drained years earlier." I crossed one leg over the other and pursed my lips, waiting for Paislee to challenge the decision so I could lash out at her further.

Instead, she took a measured and deliberate breath, like someone controlling a storm within. "And then what? He's been bound. How did that happen?"

I could work with this rage, but it might take me longer to draw out her demon.

"Mimi and Mom together were able to work up the spell. Mom finished it without asking Mimi or me if we would be okay with us being trapped here for the rest of our lives. She did it behind our backs, siphoning power from the land to strengthen her own." I scoffed and flipped my hand toward Mom. "Now look at her. Magic comes with a price."

Paislee studied me and let the silence stretch uncomfortably for several breaths. "You tricked me." Her expression darkened. "You told me Mimi was dying, but all along, it had been Mom."

I tilted my head slightly and smirked. "I knew you wouldn't come if it was Mom who was dying." I held her gaze, wordlessly asserting my dominance.

Paislee broke eye contact and shot Mom a quick glance. "That's not true, and you know it. This animosity between us is toxic." She slowly rose to her feet, uncurling and curling her fingers into fists. "I'm leaving. If you two would like to attend therapy together, maybe I will entertain this conversation again, but for now, I have to think of my mental health."

I let out a mirthless laugh. "Your mental health? Wow, you have become so soft over this past decade." I waved my hand to dismiss her. "Go back to your life, Paislee. We don't need you here."

"But she can't—" Mom sat up straight and tried to climb to her feet, but she fell back breathlessly against the cushion instead.

Paislee had already made it to the door.

I stared at my sister's back, a sharp ache blooming in my chest. I wanted her to feel my pain. "Let her leave. She's too good for us anyway."

ELEVEN

Paislee

I raced down the hallway and crashed through the door of my room. I flicked on the lights and twirled in a circle, searching every inch of the room for the ghost before slamming the door shut.

It had taken every ounce of my self-control to not wring Pandora's neck. Her words echoed in my head, each repetition reminding me I should never have returned. I wanted to forget again—forget I had a family as demented as this one.

"Damn it. Keys and phone. Where did I put those?"

A dark figure moved in my peripheral vision. My legs turned to jelly, and my knees wobbled beneath me as I slowly turned. A tall man stood in the opposite corner to my bed, near the floor-to-ceiling bookcase. His long, pointed nose turned to the side, revealing a clear outline of horns protruding from the top of his head and wings jutting from his back.

He tilted his head, then lifted his hand and waved me

toward him. I scrambled backward, running into the far wall with a hard bang. He faded in and out as he watched me, then he waved again before disappearing through the interior wall.

A stuck scream finally bubbled from my throat. I whirled in confusion, searching frantically for my belongings. I scooped up my phone from the floor. My purse lay open on the floor next to the closet door. I snatched it up and looked inside for my purple rabbit's tail, and when I saw it in there, I flew from the room.

I started my car and floored the gas pedal, peeling from the driveway with a screech.

Mimi was alive and well. Mom was alive—barely, but she was breathing and had the ability to stop whatever plagued her. I didn't understand her reluctance, but right now, I couldn't focus on the choices of my mother.

And Pandora. She had orchestrated this entire scheme to pull me back into the horrors of this estate. Ryker's fate was not my problem. I had escaped before, and I would do it again.

As I flew down the gravel road, I looked into my rearview mirror and blew out a relieved breath to see the estate growing farther away. I could leave the same way I had arrived. Mom was wrong. Maybe the three of them couldn't leave, but whatever dark force she had summoned had nothing to do with me.

I would never return here again. I loved Mom, but her insistence on staying with Ryker and subjecting us to his cruelty had driven a wedge between us that I didn't think could ever be removed. The damage, trauma, and fears from my childhood had taken me too long to heal, and I would be damned if I allowed that pain back into my life.

My heartbeat settled into a steady rhythm as the estate faded into the distance and the main road to town came into view. A sliver of guilt made me look one last time in the rearview mirror, but the hillside and trees blocked my view.

I refocused on the road ahead and screamed at the sight in front of me. The estate loomed several yards in front of me as if I had never left. I slammed on the brakes, sliding to a quick stop on the gravel road and blowing up dirt around my car.

"No, no, no, no, no," I whispered, slamming the heel of my palm on the steering wheel. "This isn't happening. This can't be happening."

Terror gripped my heart. I circled the driveway and sped back toward the main road again, ignoring the staff outside the kitchen doors watching me. Several shook their heads and pointed as if they already knew what I had just discovered. Whatever Ryker had provided for the staff, Mom and Mimi had obviously continued in his absence. The secrets were sealed within the property lines, and when crossing into town, no memory of anything extraordinary would pass.

That did not mean me. I refused to believe it.

My heart hammered inside my chest as the estate once again grew farther away, but this time I kept my eye on the approaching road. I was so close. The road had other cars on it, revealing civilization beyond Ryker's property. I had been there only yesterday, and I would not give up until I returned.

Seconds before I reached the road and the stone arches at the entrance to the property, the scene faded into a puff of air, and the estate popped back into focus. I screamed and jammed on the brakes with both feet. My hands shook as I brought them to my face and sobbed against them.

"How could this be happening?" I asked out loud, shaking my head against my hands. My breath hitched, coming in short, panicked gasps. "I have to be inside a nightmare."

A knock on the window had me biting back a scream. I wiped at my eyes and blinked at the figure on the other side of the glass.

Jersey stood outside, leaning down to look at me. "Are you okay?" He tapped lightly on the window again.

I opened the door. "No, I'm not. Did you know about this?"

"About what?" He pulled the door open wider for me and held out his hand.

I pushed it away and stood up on my own. "I can't leave, Jersey. I'm stuck again, but this time it's because of something my family did, not Ryker."

He nodded. "Oh. That."

The pit of my stomach fell. "You knew?"

"Your mom had no other choice. It was that or let them come after you." He closed his eyes and pinched the bridge of his nose. "I don't know all the details, but from what I gathered, she made an impossible decision to protect all of you."

I stared at him in shock. "And none of you could have warned me about this before I arrived?"

He lowered his hand and opened his eyes. "I tried. Trust me, I tried. You weren't reachable. And I did not think you could ever return, or else I would have done everything in my power to make sure you knew that coming home would entrap you once again."

I pressed the palm of my hand to my forehead and narrowed my eyes at him. "What do you mean I wasn't reachable?"

"Your letters went unanswered because they never

reached us. Don't you get it, Paislee?" He waved his arm out toward the property. "You weren't here, in this plane of existence. You went somewhere else."

"You're joking." A cold wave rushed over me, chilling me to the bones. "Please tell me you're joking. If that was the case, how did I return?"

He shook his head. "I don't know. There was a mixture of strange events that happened, and it all started the day you returned. It's why I came to see your family the next morning."

I bit the inside of my cheek, fighting the urge to scream. He was acting like everyone else, only providing a bare-minimum explanation, and it enraged every nerve in my body.

I stormed toward the front door. "I need a drink and a new bedroom to sleep in."

"Why a new bedroom?" he asked, jogging to catch up to me.

"Remember? There's a ghost in mine, and I am too exhausted and frustrated to have him pestering me all night." I shoved open the front door and stomped up the stairs, uncaring how loud I was being.

The door shut, and Jersey's footsteps sounded behind me.

"We can ward your room," he said when he made it to

my side near the top of the stairs.

"Look at you." I shot him a sly grin that didn't reach my eyes. There was nothing amusing about this situation. "Finally learning the magical arts."

"You've been gone for a decade. I told you a lot has changed." When we made it to the top of the stairs, he tucked his hands in the pockets of his jeans and stared at the floor. "I tried to move on, Pais. As much as I hate that Pandora tricked you into returning, I am immensely grateful to have you near me again."

"Great." I gritted my teeth. This wasn't his fault.

He held his hands up in the air in mock surrender. "I know that sounds greedy and selfish, but I've missed you. I won't apologize for it."

My heart softened, but only a smidgen. I had left without a word to anyone, even if I hadn't known where it would lead me. I wasn't going to apologize for not knowing better.

"You're forgiven." I cocked my head toward him and patted my chest. "Do you forgive me for leaving?"

He tucked a strand of hair behind my ear and smiled. "I know why you left. You had every right to leave. But yes, I forgive you."

My pulse slowed with the pause at the top of the stairs, and my thoughts returned to the conversation outside.

"Tell me about these strange events." I leaned against the railing and lifted my brows in expectation of his reply.

He leaned against the opposite wall and crossed one ankle over the other. "The entire town's lights flickered in and out the day you arrived. I had volunteered at the fire station that day, and the calls rolled in one after another. Sightings of ghostly figures, people appearing and then vanishing, and lights that exploded along the road toward the estate." His eyes glossed over as if deep in thought. "I spent the entire day and night chasing down ghosts myself and coming up empty at every turn."

"Nothing? You didn't find any evidence to why those events happened?"

He pursed his lips and moved his head in a slow, deliberate no. "As quickly as it started, it ended. I worried that Ryker had found a way out and somehow had split the fabric of reality. I came by to check on your family and make sure that hadn't happened. Instead, I found you."

"And now I'm being haunted." I pushed away from the railing. "Doesn't seem like a coincidence."

He closed the distance enough for me to feel the warmth from his body yet not close enough for me to touch. His fingers twitched at his sides before he stuffed them back in his pockets, a poor attempt to keep them from betraying him.

I grinned at his behavior, then rose on my toes and planted a kiss on his cheek. "How do we ward my room from a ghost?" I asked, pulling one of his hands from his pocket to hold as we started walking again.

His fingers entwined with mine. "First, how do you know you have a ghost? Maybe it isn't a ghost."

I tapped my mouth while swinging our arms between us, thinking back to when the figure stood above me. It had faded in and out repeatedly, like a beat strumming in and out of my reality. Jersey said I hadn't been here, whatever that meant. Maybe this ghost was not supposed to be here either.

I stopped in front of my room and stared at the door, then turned toward him. I wasn't ready to go inside. "It's an entity. Does it matter what it is?"

"Not necessarily," he replied, opening my bedroom door and looking around. "It would help to know exactly what it is so I can banish it entirely. Or we could have a séance and ask it what it wants."

"That sounds like a hard no to me." I flopped onto my bed and rolled onto my side to watch him. "I don't think the ghost meant to harm or scare me, but I don't want it in my room. Whatever he wants with me can be discussed in another area of the estate."

"Fair enough. I'll have it warded after dinner." He walked around the room, mumbling under his breath as he visited each corner.

I watched him in silence, admiring his whiskers and late-twenties physique. He had grown up in all the right places, and I had to admit, I enjoyed the view. His gray T-shirt left little to the imagination, with his chest and arm muscles pressing against the fabric. His dark-wash boot-cut jeans gripped his quads and hamstrings, providing me with all the filthy thoughts I had deprived myself of for too many years.

Jersey cleared his throat. "You're staring."

I slid my gaze up to meet his. "Can you blame me?" I batted my lashes at him as a longing for him to be closer whispered through me.

"Do you want me to focus on your ghost or on you?" He sauntered my way.

I laughed and waved him away. "The ghost. Maybe we can focus on one another after I figure out how to leave this place again."

He leaned down, pressing his palms on the mattress, and kissed my nose. "I'm holding you to that. This time, I want to join you."

Desire ignited within me, and a sudden ache of need gripped my core. I slid my legs in between his arms, then pulled him closer.

"Actually, I've changed my mind. Focus on me instead," I whispered, wrapping my legs around his waist.

A smile pinched his cheeks. He licked his lips, and his gaze flitted to my mouth, then he mashed ours together. I melted against him, forgetting all about the ghost, the curse, and my lunatic twin sister trying to upheave the peace I had worked so hard to obtain.

TWELVE

Pandora

Guilt gripped me the moment I woke.

Mimi remained tethered to her room, and I hadn't checked on her since I left her yesterday. The spell was not the most stable, and I knew it wouldn't last past the twenty-four hours, but the thought of her being secluded made me ill.

I rolled out of bed and slid my feet into my slippers, then pulled on a hoodie over my tank top.

The kitchen staff had completed breakfast by the time I made it to the dining room. Paislee was sitting on the far end of the table with her knees pulled up against her chest and a mug of steaming coffee in her hands.

She slipped me a quick glance, before refocusing on the view outside. "Morning, traitor."

"Go to hell, deserter." I stuck my tongue out at her.

I grabbed a plate and piled it with Mimi's favorites, then filled a glass with orange juice before leaving. The energy hung heavily in that room, and I knew what I was about to do would definitely label me a traitor for life. Shame corroded my insides, but I gritted my teeth and tightened my grip on the plate, forcing myself to think of anything but the freeing results of my actions.

I had never seen the ocean, and in a few short days, I would be listening to the surf hit the sand. That was what I needed, time with my feet buried in the sand and the sun baking my skin.

Outside Mimi's suite, I murmured the few words needed to temporarily undo the spell. I cradled the glass between my ribs and elbow to open the door, then propped it open with my foot.

"Mimi," I called before entering. "I have breakfast for—"

Paislee ducked under my elbow and shoved the door open fully. "Why are you bringing Mimi breakfast? Is she ill?"

The desperation written across her face nearly stirred a sense of pity in me.

"Get out," I snapped, setting the glass and plate on the nearest surface. I stormed after her.

Mimi rounded the corner from her bedroom. "What's all the commotion?" She glowered at me, wrapping her silk robe tighter around her waist. "Letting me out early? Why? So you can strangle me next?"

Paislee whirled around to confront me, her expression melting into a scowl. "What is she talking about?"

"Get a grip." I hurried back to the plate of food and drink, then showed it to Mimi. "I knew you would want a real breakfast. I brought your favorites."

"What for? Did you mess something up and need me to fix it for you?" Mimi took the plate and glass and huffed at me. "Get out. Paislee, you might want to leave too, so she doesn't trap you in here as well." Mimi stopped suddenly and turned to look at me again. She laughed. "Well, well, well, this must be your thing. A carbon copy of Ryker. He taught you better than I anticipated."

Paislee shook her head. "What is happening?"

"Your twin has cooked up something with Ryker and doesn't want me to tell my daughter about it." Her expression hardened. "She bound me to my suite at lunchtime yesterday and won't let me out for twenty-four hours. I guess at that point, she will have completed whatever traitorous act she is planning."

Mimi set her plate down and took a drink of orange juice.

"Why are you doing this?" Paislee grabbed my arm, squeezing it so tight, her fingernails dug into my skin. "Isn't it bad enough you tricked me into returning?"

"God, Pais, you are insufferable. Boo-hoo on your

93

predicament." I pried her fingers from my arm and stomped toward Mimi. "Cry me a river. Both of you."

Mimi raised her brow at my advancement but did not flinch. I choked back the ball of fury rising in my throat.

"What about me, Mimi? Do you even care what happens with me? Or are you content with watching me wither away in this estate with you and Mom?" I yelled, inches from her face. "Ryker at least had the dignity to let me find my own way. That's more than I can say about you."

Mimi lifted the glass of orange juice to her lips, hiding a soft sigh behind it.

Red hot rage tore through my veins. I grabbed her glass and hurled it across the room. It shattered against the far wall.

"Dora!" Paislee shouted at me. "Stop it. What do you gain from keeping us all here? And what does Mimi mean you are cooking something up with Ryker?" Her hand curled around my shoulder.

I shoved off her hold on me and threw her a dirty look. "Stop. Touching. Me. For fuck's sake, Paislee. Leave your hands off me. Ryker doesn't exist anymore. Mimi is insane."

"She's lying," Mimi said, taking a step backward. "Your mom bound him in the—"

"Stop!" I snarled, giving Mimi a quick push before thinking about my actions.

Mimi toppled backward, knocking over her plate of food and splaying it over the furniture. Her arms flailed, and Paislee leaped past me to catch Mimi, but her head struck the edge of the coffee table with an eerie snap. She landed on her back next to us. A choked gargle noise spewed from her mouth, then her eyes rolled back and her limbs went limp.

"Mimi!" Paislee shrieked, collapsing next to her. She shook Mimi's shoulders. "Wake up. Please, Mimi. Wake up."

I circled Mimi and lowered to the ground opposite Paislee. I wanted to curl up in shame, but this wasn't the time to fold. Ryker's promise fluttered within me, and knowing my freedom was around the corner was enough motivation to keep up the charade.

Paislee stared at me in horror. "What happened to you, Dora? Why would you do this?"

I shrugged to hide my concern for Mimi. "I guess I've become the ruthless villain you have always believed me to be."

"Villain?" She scrunched her face in confusion. "This is ridiculous. I never thought you were a villain."

"You left me, Paislee." I wiped Mimi's hair from her

face, then searched her head for injuries.

"I didn't mean to leave you. It's not like we were ever able to walk in and out of Ryker's property before that day." She spoke softly, her voice fraying at the edges, barely above a whisper. "It was a fluke chance. Don't you understand that?"

I pulled my hands away from Mimi and looked up at my sister. "No, I don't. You didn't want to be challenged that day and threw a big tantrum with Ryker. When I wouldn't leave you alone, you found a way to slip away and left me to face Ryker's wrath alone."

"No, I didn't—not on purpose at least. Is this what this is all about?" She pressed her fingers against Mimi's wrist. "You're out to seek revenge because I didn't take you with me?"

I swatted her hand away from Mimi. "She's not dead, you idiot. You left me. And that is the only reason I hate you. I should have mattered more to you, but I didn't."

THIRTEEN

Paislee

My shoulders stiffened as if bracing for impact. "It always has to be about you, doesn't it? I can check Mimi's pulse if I want."

I pressed my fingers to the side of Mimi's neck and held my breath until I felt her faint pulse. Relief washed over me. I pulled out my phone from my back pocket and dialed 9-1-1.

"It won't work." Pandora reached behind Mimi's head, and when she pulled it back, it was covered in blood.

"No, no, no," I whispered as the walls around me seemed to close in.

The phone rang dozens of times. I pulled it away and made sure I'd dialed correctly. The numbers 9-1-1 glared back at me. I placed the phone back to my ear. It continued to ring.

"Why aren't they answering?" I grumbled quietly, looking at my phone again.

"I told you." Pandora wiped her hand down her

hoodie, then scratched her brow with her other hand. "I'll go fetch Cassie. She always knows what to do."

I ended the call and set my phone next to Mimi. "We have to stop the bleeding first." I jumped to my feet and bolted for the bathroom.

The lavender scent hit me in the face when I opened the door to Mimi's powder room. I waved my hand in my face to dispel the smell, opening cupboards to find towels. I gathered several in my arms and raced back to Mimi.

Pandora was gone, but that didn't surprise me. I carefully lifted Mimi's head and slipped several washcloths underneath, then pressed them against her skull, hoping I had the right spot.

With my free hand, I opened my phone again. If the staff from the town could come and go, I bet I could reach someone outside the property lines.

I clicked on the first social media application. I didn't know who I could contact, being that all my acquaintances were the few people I had worked with or lived near over the past decade. What could they even do about my situation?

They could call the police for me.

I clicked on Amanda's name at the top and typed in my message.

Help please. I'm home with my family and my

grandma has been hurt, but I can't get through to the first responders. Will you call 911 for me? I'll send you my address.

I pressed send, but nothing happened. Even after pressing it again, the message stayed in place. I gritted my teeth. I clicked back to the main page and refreshed it. The same posts popped up that had been there several days earlier. I refreshed again, and once again, only older posts were showcased.

I hurled my phone. "Help!" I hollered, pounding my fist on the wall. "Please, help!"

The silence dragged on for what felt like ages as I changed the cloth I had pressed against Mimi's head. I lifted my free hand and found it trembling. Sheer panic pounded at my chest.

What was taking Pandora so long?

The door swung open. Mom stepped inside the room, holding onto the frame for support. Her skin was devoid of color, and the whites of her eyes had a yellow hue. A cold chill ran down my spine as she slowly made it to my side, her feet sliding along the floor.

"What happened?" she asked, nearly collapsing breathless next to me.

"Pandora shoved Mimi, and she fell and hit her head. And then Pandora left to find some help." I pulled the blood-soaked washcloths out from underneath Mimi.

Mom swallowed hard, rubbing her eyes with her knuckles. "Let's roll her to her side. I need to have a better view."

I followed Mom's lead and gently rolled Mimi to her left side. Mom settled cross-legged behind Mimi's head with a flashlight. She moved Mimi's silver locks around until she reached the section hiding the injury and pressed a clean cloth against it.

Her gaze flitted to meet mine. "That foolish girl. What were they arguing about this time?"

"Pandora had Mimi locked in her room since lunch yesterday."

Mom pressed her free hand against her temple and closed her eyes. "Why would Dora do that?"

"I don't know exactly." I scooted closer and helped Mom put pressure on the wound. "Mimi said Pandora was cooking up something with Ryker, but—"

"She is what?" Mom sat up straight and shot a look at the door. "How? When?"

I threw my hands in the air, almost pulling the towels from Mimi's head. "You tell me. I walked in on your messy ordeal, and I still haven't pieced together the what, who, how, or when of anything. All I know is I can't leave and there's a ghost wandering the estate and my family is at each other's throats, but none of them can tell me the truth."

"There's a ghost in the estate?" Mom shot me a sideways look before checking the cloth. The blood flow had slowed. "It's barely a nick. These head wounds are usually more blood than injury, but I will have to ask Cassie to bring the physician in tonight."

"Hi, ma'am," Cassie said behind us as if summoned. "Let me help."

Cassie hurried to Mom's side and leaned down, curling her hands under Mom's underarms. She lifted Mom to her feet and led her to the couch.

"Thank you, Cassie. Will you bring the doctor?" Mom sank to the cushion.

Cassie nodded feverishly. "Yes, of course. I will check your mother first."

I shifted out of the way, seeing Pandora enter the suite. She leaned against the wall, nibbling on her fingernails and watching us all closely. Her long hair hung in front of her, blocking most of her face from view, but I wanted to believe there was remorse in her expression. Pandora's vindictive nature had been a defense mechanism when we were children but not her true character.

I rose to my feet. "Dora, I need better answers. You told me Mimi was ill and that Ryker had no control over the estate or us any longer. Mimi isn't ill, and Ryker is somewhere close. Why did you lie?"

Her gaze drifted from Mimi to me, and she pushed away from the wall. "I told you. You wouldn't come if it was Mom who was sick." She circled me and stopped a few feet from Mimi, watching Cassie dab at the head wound.

"That's not entirely true, and you know it. I would come for Mom." I sank to the edge of the table and tapped my fingers against it. "But that's not the point. Ryker—"

Pandora leaned in close to Mimi and whispered something to Cassie I couldn't hear.

"Stay away from her," Mom hissed between clenched teeth. "You've done enough damage."

"Me?" Pandora stood up straight and pointed at herself in mock horror. "We are in this situation because of you."

"I've apologized more times than I can count. What I did was done out of fear for your sister and for our lives." Mom trembled as she tried to rise to her feet. She fell back on the cushion with a soft cry. "He wouldn't have stopped at me. He would have—"

"Then it's her fault." Pandora pointed at me with malice in her tone. "She only thinks of herself."

"Your mother's injury is small, but I suspect she will have a concussion and we shouldn't take a chance with her head," Cassie said as she stood. She wiped her hands down her pant legs. "We must move her to her bed. Then I will go for the doctor." She looked at me. "Will you help me?"

I rushed to her side. "Of course."

"Of course," I heard Pandora sarcastically mumble under her breath.

Mimi stirred and moaned.

"It will be best to lift her from her underarms, similar to how I did with your mother. We can each take a side." Cassie leaned down and wiped Mimi's hair from her face. "Esther, we are taking you to your bed so you can be comfortable."

Mimi moaned again, but she slowly nodded.

I took the opposite side of Cassie, and we hoisted Mimi to her feet. Pandora watched from a few feet away without an offer to help.

"Pandora, you should be ashamed of yourself," Mom muttered.

"I'm ashamed of you," Pandora clipped back. "We are cursed because of Paislee's choices, and I'm not going to apologize for choosing myself."

"No, that's not true. We were cursed long before Paislee escaped. Ryker did far—"

"It's always Ryker's fault, isn't it? You can never take

responsibility for anything."

Cassie and I slowly steered Mimi toward her bedroom doors, leaving the arguing behind us in Mimi's sitting room. I strained to hear their conversation, but they kept their voices low, and with Mimi leaning heavily against me, I couldn't focus on their words.

"She will be fine, miss," Cassie whispered as we laid Mimi on her bed. "The doctor knows your family well and will take great care of your grandmother."

I laid Mimi's arms to her sides and nodded. "Thank you, Cassie. I'm sorry my family has created such a mess."

Cassie gave me a curt nod before leaving the room.

I sank to the edge of the bed and swept a lock of hair from Mimi's face. She murmured but did not open her eyes.

Sorrow closed my throat as I recognized the damage I had caused by disappearing. My family had paid for my choice to walk through that light and not come back when I'd had the chance. Almost every memory before I left felt like a blade—cold, sharp, and unforgiving. But I should have stayed.

Now, Mom faced death without explanation, and I suspected it was because of this secret the three of them held about Ryker. When I was young, Mom had acted as if she'd chosen to be with Ryker, but maybe there was more to her past than what had been disclosed.

I kissed Mimi on the forehead, then rose to my feet and drew in a long, deliberate breath. I intended on finding out the truth before our lives truly crumbled together.

FOURTEEN

Pandora

I stared after Paislee and Mimi, hating myself for what I had done but refusing to do anything to help.

"We have to fix this," Mom said, croaking out the words as if they were painful.

I turned to face her. "No, *you* have to fix this, Mom. I was young and innocent and didn't deserve to have this burden placed on my shoulders. You are the one who needs to fix the damage your decision made on this family."

Her shoulders hunched over the visible weight of exhaustion. "There is more to it than that."

"Always is. You never tell me more though." Hot anger rushed through my veins. I slid open the nearest window to cool my skin. "I'm just expected to trust you, but now that I'm older, I am hyperaware of the manipulation. You don't deserve my sympathy for what Ryker has done to you and Mimi when you are literally repeating his actions."

"Not even close." Mom scooted to the edge of her seat, her face flushing red. "Why would I ever disclose the worst of my trauma to you? Why can't you just believe I am protecting you from experiencing what I have gone through?"

"Because it's unbelievable." I picked up a book on the side table and ran my fingers down its spine. "Ryker might be controlling, but he never locked me away."

Mom laughed. "But he did. He locked us all away from the world beyond this property. Not to mention—" She grimaced as if she was in pain. "Damn it. Never mind."

"And there you go again. Being cryptic." My guts curled in disgust. "I'm expected to understand without being told any more details."

"The details cannot be said!" Mom cried, pressing her palms against her eyes. "How many times do I need to say this to you?"

"Fuck you," I spat at her as Paislee came into view. I glared at my sister. "And fuck you as well."

I hurled the book at Paislee, then picked up a glass dragon figurine and chucked it at her as well. The book landed behind Paislee with a thud, but the figurine struck her hip bone. She yelped and curled in on herself as the figurine tumbled beside her without breaking.

Paislee's quivering hand grabbed at her hip, her red-rimmed eyes glowering at me. "What was that for?"

The pain in her expression did not faze me. I flipped her off before wrapping my hand around the base of the lamp. I ripped the cord from the plug in the wall and flung it at my sister. It hit her on the side of her head, then crashed to the floor. The bulb shattered.

Paislee stumbled backward, pressing her palm against her ear.

"Stop it," Mom cried, pulling herself to a standing position and taking a step toward me. "Dora, please stop! Let's talk about this before someone gets really hurt."

I grabbed at the roots of my hair and screamed in her direction. "No! No more talking!"

The side table lifted easily. I heaved it into my arms and flung it toward Paislee, hoping it would hurt her so badly, she wouldn't have any other choice but to follow me.

The table landed inches in front of Paislee. One leg twisted and another one splintered in half from the impact, but the best reaction came from my sister. Her face darkened, and her nostrils flared as she sucked in a sharp breath. A bright crimson bloomed on her cheeks, and she turned her hate-filled gaze toward me.

"You better run, bitch, or I'm going to kill you," she hissed, her words sharp enough to cut. She shoved the table out of her way and stalked forward, each step deliberate and heavy.

"Don't, Paislee." Mom held her hand out toward Paislee.

But Paislee didn't seem to even hear her as her gaze cut right through me like a sharp blade.

I ripped off my hoodie and shifted into my raven form before she reached me. I croaked at them and flew from the room, delighted that my plan was finally coming together. The thrill of her anger rushed through me like a drug, and the deep satisfaction from witnessing her fury ignited my drive to finish what I had started.

Until she shifted, I would not be able to obtain what Ryker's spell required.

I soared high, then circled back around and saw Mom and Paislee at the window. Mom waved for me to return, holding a firm hand on Paislee's shoulder, but I knew they would both strangle me if I returned. Every one of Mom's muscles was taut with silent fury.

I cawed at them, flying to and fro in front of the window, daring Paislee to follow. After several minutes, she shook her head and turned her back toward me. Mom waved again. I flew closer, turning in a circle near the window, cawing repeatedly. The staff peered up at me, unfazed by my cries.

How many times had I thrown these fits since Paislee had left? No one cared any more. Frustration bit at my mind, and my patience was unraveling thread by thread.

I shot away from the window, flying toward the tunnel doorway near the forest. The thick brush came into view, and I settled onto the ground nearby, then shifted back to my human form.

I shoved the door open, and the light flickered on, revealing an empty corridor.

"Ryker," I yelled, stepping across the threshold.

He appeared out of thin air a few feet in front of me, his figure blurry and fading in and out. When he manifested completely, his usual sharp, high cheekbones appeared expanded and grotesque with crusty lesions peppered across his face. Dark horns adorned the crown of his head, twisting backward along his scalp. I backed away instinctively, disbelief weighing down my spine.

"Where have you been?" A vein in his forehead bulged as his breath came in ragged gasps. "I have warned you, Pandora."

He faded again, then popped back into view, appearing normal once more.

I inhaled a sharp breath, not sure what or who I was looking at anymore. My mind scrambled for a foothold, searching for something solid to hold onto. I blinked slow_y—once, twice—as I refocused on him, feeling grateful he had not changed to whatever that creature had been.

"I've been busy handling your requirements." I wrapped my hand around the frame of the door. "The ritual will happen tonight. Paislee has refused to shift, but I will make it happen today."

"You. Are. So. Predictable. Lazy and a fucking waste of my time." His voice cracked like a whip, each syllable a warning.

"Do you want out or not?" I adjusted my sleeves and fiddled with my watch, anything to avoid his eyes. "I can find another way."

"There isn't any other way." His glare transformed into an arrogant smile.

He noticed my unease. I dropped my arms to my sides.

"Get it done, Dora. I've grown impatient with your delays. If you want this to work for both of us, it must happen tonight."

Was it too late to stop this? The air in my lungs felt thin, swallowed up by the crushing weight of dread. "And what if it's not done tonight?"

"Then I will ensure your family's suffering after you leave." He tilted his head in amusement. "You have no moves left. If you want to leave my home, you must do it

111

my way."

"I hate you," I hissed, backing up over the threshold. "Be ready. It will be done tonight." I turned to leave but stopped in my tracks. "And you're welcome, asshole." Then I yanked the massive door shut.

If I had more time, I might have found another way, but I had already put his plan into action. And after my behavior in Mimi's suite, I doubted I would find forgiveness.

I felt like I could explode from the anger pressing against my ribs like a caged animal. My family and Ryker deserved one another. Once this was completed, I would never look back on this place again.

FIFTEEN

Paitlee

"Why didn't you want me to go after her?" I asked, standing in the middle of Mimi's sitting room and staring at the closed window.

Mom coughed before sliding onto the nearest seat. "She was antagonizing you on purpose. I'm not sure why she's being this way, but the past year, she has been more secretive about her life and bitter about her circumstances." She leaned back with a sigh. "I don't trust her motives right now."

I kneeled in front of Mom and squeezed her calf. "I need answers, Mom. What happened while I was away? Why have you stayed for so long? And why have you trapped Ryker?"

Tears pooled silently in Mom's eyes, and she closed them. The tears slipped down her cheeks in small rivulets.

"I've known Ryker for over a hundred years. My mother knew him first and befriended him long before he used his human form to manipulate the world." She opened her eyes and wiped her cheeks with both hands. "Ryker is not who he appears to be, but he has been able to hold me and Mimi for decades now. It all started with the king and his daughter and the three pesky fairies."

I grabbed her hands. "They really did a number on you, didn't they?"

"The story Ryker told you is a lie." Her fingers trailed down the side of my face, where I had been struck by the figurine. "She really hurt you. We should have the doctor examine you."

"I'll be fine. I always knew the story wasn't accurate." I pulled her hand away from my face. "You don't have to explain that to me."

"My history is complicated, Paislee. How you know me is not who I am." She dragged her fingers along the arm of the chair, lingering like she didn't know what else to say.

"What do you mean by that?" I rocked on my knees and rubbed at the knot forming on my hip. The ache radiated into my thigh, but I bit back the pain so I could focus on Mom.

She watched me carefully, noticing every movement I made.

"I promise, Mom. I will be fine. It's going to hurt later, but I'll manage for now." I curled my toes under and pushed myself to my feet. "Tell me what's going on with you. What do you mean by how I know you isn't who you are?"

She patted my hands and scooted to the edge of the chair. "I hope to find a way to tell you everything. And when I do, I promise you will know the entire truth." Her gaze drifted behind me. "We need to check on her."

I sighed and rubbed my palms together to warm them. "I'll check on her. You rest, and I'll be back."

She nodded and leaned back on the cushion with a soft sigh. "Thank you."

On my way to Mimi's bedroom, movement near the doorway caught my eye. I stepped backward and leaned around the corner of the wall to see better. "Pandora?"

The shadow stepped closer. Its height nearly touched the top of the doorframe, and a sharp tip of a horn came into view.

"Who are you?" I asked, flooded with sudden helplessness—the not knowing gnawed at me like an itch I couldn't reach.

A visible smile spread on its face, and it turned to reveal its long, pointed nose that reminded me of the man from the elevator. He beckoned me closer.

Oh. My. God. It *was* the man from the elevator.

I slapped a hand over my mouth and whirled to look at

Mom. She stared back at me with wide eyes.

"Who are you talking to?" she asked, her gaze flitting to the doorway and back to me.

"You can't see him?" I jabbed my thumb toward the doorway.

The figure had moved into the hallway, but he stared back at me as if inviting me to follow him.

"Mom, I know you're tired, but you need to go to Mimi and stay with her." I jerked my head toward the bedroom. "I'll be back soon."

"Paislee, whoever is there, don't trust them. Ryker might have found a way to reach—"

I heard her move toward me, but I waved a dismissive hand. "Stay here, Mom." Then I raced from the room, following the quickly retreating ghost.

After making several turns down different hallways, the figure glanced over its shoulder to make sure I continued to follow him. He faded slightly, then formed into the man from the elevator, throwing all my doubts out the window. Before I could call after him, he pivoted and slipped through a closed door that led to a section of the estate I had never been allowed in.

Ryker's wing.

I stood in front of the double doors, squeezing my fists repeatedly. A cold sweat trickled down my spine, leaving the back of my shirt damp and clinging to my skin. Mom wouldn't take the chance by binding Ryker to his wing. I knew that, but trepidation swam violently in my gut anyway. I had been forbidden to ever enter, and the child who'd run these halls knew better than to test her limits inside the house. Outside, the trees had protected me. Inside had been Ryker's domain.

The doors creaked open, and my heart leaped into my throat. I took several quick steps backward and, with bated breath, watched for any sign of Ryker or his men.

Darkness seeped out with the drapes pulled and the lights extinguished. Shadows stretched and twisted, whispering secrets in the dark. After several terrifying minutes, no one else appeared and the ghost had vanished. I tiptoed forward and peeked inside the entry room. The furniture had been covered, but the carpet had been vacuumed recently, showing some kind of life inside of the suite.

For some strange reason, that provided some comfort. With trembling fingers, I reached over and flipped up the light switch. Light flooded the room, revealing the tall ceilings and art covering the walls.

But there wasn't a ghost or elevator man in sight.

I pressed my hands against my chest. "Hello?"

Every creak of the floor sent a bolt of terror thundering

through my chest.

I took several more hesitant steps, passing through the entryway, and made my way into a large sitting room. A bar filled with various liquors stood at one end of the room and a grand piano at the other, with several chairs and couches in the middle.

The dark figure shifted out of the shadows, and the man from the elevator came into full view. We stared at one another for several breaths, frozen by surprise, relief, or fear. I wasn't quite sure. The silence wasn't comforting but instead hung thick and heavy.

"It's really you," I finally whispered, my breath catching in my throat. "How? Did you follow me here?"

His facial features faded in and out, and his mouth moved as if he were speaking, but I couldn't hear anything.

I tapped on my ear. "I can't hear you."

He turned to the side, and the horns on top of his head appeared, then faded out again. I stared in dumbstruck disbelief as he pointed at the liquor cabinet.

I crept forward a few feet and peered over the counter. A sighing breeze caught my attention, and I turned back to face him.

"Stop her from d—" he whispered before fully disappearing.

SIXTEEN

Pandora

I slipped in through the patio door, paying no attention to the maid cleaning the room. She bowed and averted her eyes, but I really didn't care who saw me.

No more delays. Fresh energy fueled me. This would be done today.

I sprinted up the stairs and pushed past another maid when I rounded the corner to my room.

"Move it." My words were short and clipped like broken glass.

She grunted but kept her distance. The staff could come and go from the property as they pleased, and it irritated me beyond measure. The connection between their existence and ours had been established by Ryker before I could remember, and the how frustrated me. The town stood so close but was completely out of my reach, and most residents pretended we didn't exist. The few who visited did not stay long, aside from the staff. They were loyal to Mom or Mimi or maybe Ryker. Who knew.

No one was loyal to me.

I yanked on a pair of old jogger pants and a dark shirt. My black runaway bag sat on my bed, waiting for the moment I left. The few possessions I had wanted were secure, leaving the majority of the room untouched. My journal and several important books had been folded into a small selection of my clothes, keeping them protected from prying eyes.

The tiny fridge on my bathroom counter held the three vials of blood. One from me, one from Mom, and the last from Mimi. I only needed Paislee's, and the show could finally begin.

I was so close, I could taste freedom.

I wandered around my room, taking in the paintings of oceans and horses that I'd once asked Ryker to hang. He had been controlling and possessive, but he'd never failed to give me whatever I wanted when I was younger. There was a twisted kind of satisfaction he seemed to take in playing the role of the doting father figure—and I had learned to use it to my advantage whenever I could.

The green-and-lilac furniture complemented the splashes of oranges and yellows, along with the four-poster bed and the sheer curtains that hung from each post. I had felt like a princess lying in this bed and had spent many nights imagining my life once I gained my freedom.

I shoved the needle into my pocket and patted it before leaving the room.

"Faislee!" I yelled when I reached the main hallway.

At the staircase, I looked below. Another maid held a duster, using it to clean the bookcases outside the entryway.

"Have you seen Paislee?" I called down to her.

Her gaze darted around the room in confusion, then she tilted her head and looked upward. Her gaze met mine, and she visibly shuddered.

"Well, have you?" I asked again. My foot bounced repeatedly against the carpet.

"No, no I haven't, miss." She bowed her head, then hurried out of sight.

"Miss," a female called from above me.

I moved to the base of the stairs and looked up at the maid I had run into earlier.

"She was up here, last I saw. Near his wing." She pursed her lips as if mentioning Ryker would curse her.

"Good God. You are all so weak." I flew up the stairs. "Did she go inside Ryker's suite?" I crossed my arms over my chest, the way Ryker did when he was angry with me.

The redheaded young woman nodded and skittered backward several feet, giving me a wide berth. "The doors opened without her touching them. Then she went inside."

My lips parted slightly, caught between a question and silence. That wasn't like Paislee. She always followed the rules of the house. Only in the forest had she disobeyed Ryker.

I walked past the maid, paying her no attention, and rounded the corner that led to Ryker's suite. The corridor lay in darkness, but the french doors were cracked with light streaming through the opening.

As I inched the door open with my toes, a rustling from somewhere inside caught my ear. It sounded like someone was moving glass bottles together or rummaging through the glasses.

I tiptoed through the entryway and into the sitting room and found Paislee on the far end, pulling out all the liquor bottles from the cabinets and shelves. Her lips moved as if she was speaking to herself, but whatever was being said was too quiet to hear.

"What are you doing in here?" I asked, walking toward her.

Paislee shrieked and jumped, turning to face me in one movement. "Good God! Pandora, you scared me."

"I would be scared too. You shouldn't be going through Ryker's belongings." I leaned on my elbows over the counter and peered at the floor on the other side. The side of her face was bruised with a forming goose egg pressing out above her ear. "Are you binge drinking?"

Dozens of bottles were strewn across the floor.

"No, I am looking for Mom's cure." She waved her hands around erratically. "The tall man with the horns asked me to stop Mom from dying. He had pointed at these cabinets and kept muttering—"

I held out my hand toward her. "Hold it. Wait." I couldn't help but let out an amused laugh, despite my hatred for my sister. "A tall man with horns? Can we rewind to that part?" I didn't mention the horns I had seen protruding from Ryker's head, nor the ones I knew Jersey had. It would have ruined all the fun.

"It's not funny." She scowled at me, and two lines formed between her brows. "He faded away, and now I'm trying to figure out what he meant. I think Ryker has something in here that will save her."

"But why would a tall man with horns want to save Mom?" I choked back another laugh.

"I don't know." She shook her head, looking around at the mess she had made. "He confronted me in the parking garage at the hotel, after riding the elevator with me and listening to some other man drone on about being stuck in an elevator. He mentioned something about making the best choice for myself and then suddenly he was here." Her fingers raked through her long curls, and she winced from pulling on the injured side of her head. "I know it sounds crazy, but it's all true."

I wanted her to stop talking nonsense, but my curiosity got the best of me. "Did he have horns in the elevator? Why would you talk to someone like that?"

"No, he didn't. Good grief, Dora. Either I'm losing my mind, or a horned ghost is haunting me." She rubbed her eyes, then clenched her hands into fists and tapped them against her temples.

"Insanity is always the better choice." I rounded the counter and peered into the lower cabinets. Dozens of other bottles sat at the back. "It appears that Ryker had a drinking or hoarding problem. I doubt there is anything in here that would save Mom. Unless…"

"Unless what?" Paislee leaned over and looked in the cabinet as well.

A warm wave of mirth rolled through me. "Unless she wants to drink herself to her grave. It's messy but will do the job."

"Are you for real!" Paislee hollered, shoving me in the arm.

I fell backward, stumbling over my feet before landing on my backside. "Bitch!" I jumped up and stormed toward her. "What's your problem?"

"You're my problem!" she screamed, grabbing the

neck of a vodka bottle and waving it between us. "You've been nothing but a horrible person since I arrived. First, tricking me to come back, knowing I wouldn't be able to leave, and then rubbing it in my face that Mom is dying. Then to top off this lunacy, you attack me in Mimi's suite." She backed away from me.

"Golly geez, poor Paislee." I followed her around the counter, balling my hands into fists. "Let's do this. You want to fight, let's take it outside, and do it the right way."

She stopped in her tracks and straightened her stature, her eyes lighting up with sudden interest. "What's the right way?"

My lips curled into a sneer, my eyes burning with fury. "The way Ryker taught us."

"You never could beat me, Dora." She shook her head and backed away farther, holding up her free hand in mock surrender and setting the vodka bottle onto the side table. "It's not a fair fight."

My adrenaline skyrocketed and I flew at her, jabbing my fist into her chin. I nailed her so hard, I heard a bone crack. "Don't you dare tell me I can't win. I've had ten years to practice, while you cowered in a reality where you couldn't be reached." I huffed in her face as my chest rose and fell heavily with each breath.

Paislee cowered away from me, moaning and covering

125

the other side of her face. She glanced over at me and, with her other hand, wiped away her blood and tears. They smeared across her face. "Fine," she hissed. "Let's do this."

SEVENTEEN

Paislee

Pandora gathered several bottles of liquor in her arms, then raced ahead of me. Her singing voice carried throughout the estate as she took a swig of vodka and threw me a wicked smile. She hurled the bottle down the hallway, and it shattered near a surprised staff member.

The woman shrieked and jumped out of the way before sprinting in the opposite direction.

"You're all weak!" Pandora yelled after her.

She opened a bottle of whiskey, skipping down the first flight of steps. The brown liquid seeped down her chin as she took several shots, then she leaned over the railing and dropped the bottle. The crash below us reverberated around us and the sound of running feet filled the space.

I picked up my speed. "Pandora, this is unnecessary. Leave the house staff out of this."

She whirled in a circle on and grinned up at me. "This is all necessary, dear sister. All of it. And you can all go to the final steps to the second floor hell for all I care."

She bounded down the next flight of stairs before I made it to the second floor. The smell of whiskey permeated the air as I walked past the broken glass and puddles of liquid. When I reached the stairs, Pandora had another open bottle of liquor with the opening in her mouth. She chugged several gulps, then tossed the bottle over her shoulder.

It shattered on the stone floor, and the glass slid in every direction.

I groaned and ran down the stairs, noticing the setting sun from the west windows.

At the bottom of the stairs, I paused and turned toward the bright evening light. The day had faded away quickly. Most of the staff had left, aside from a handful of stragglers completing the last of their work. The smell of dinner lingered in the air, and I realized I hadn't eaten since breakfast, but my stomach revolted from the thought of food.

I hated what I was about to do with the remaining staff still here, but Pandora had left me no choice.

I stepped outside, and a rush of the late-summer air greeted me. I peeled off my jacket and let it drop to the porch. Pandora was halfway to the forest entrance. She wanted me to hunt her the way Ryker had taught me. It had been his cruel game and the only time we received his permission to venture into the forest.

The memories jabbed at my mind, and nausea rolled in my stomach. Pandora knew I hated this. She knew I did not want to wake my demon, but we needed to find some balance again, and if this was the way I could reach her, then so be it.

Someone from the kitchen staff walked around the corner of the estate, holding a basket of tablecloths. She skidded to a halt when she noticed me.

"My apologies." She bowed her head and took a step backward.

"I'm not Pandora. You should leave." I gestured toward the house. "Get your things and leave. Tell the rest of the staff to go as well."

She gave me a curt nod and jogged past me. "Yes, miss."

I watched her enter the house and close the door, then I heard shouting from inside. I wanted to give them as much time as possible before transforming. After a long inhale, I followed Pandora.

The demon stirred inside me as I coaxed her awake for the first time in a decade. I greeted her warmly and felt her power surge through every muscle in my body. The energy flooded my veins, igniting the flames I had been holding back for far too long.

Then I surrendered control and welcomed the euphoria that filled my core. My head stretched to the tops of the doorways, and I extended my massive wings, relishing in the relief that washed through me from being restrained for so long. The fog from my transformation billowed out around me, slipping through the vegetation and fluttering with the breeze.

I let out an ear-piercing roar.

The greens and darkest blacks of my scales glistened against the setting sun, illuminating my position. I lumbered toward the forest, allowing my colors to fade to the shade of the vegetation and transform me into a nearly translucent creature. I wouldn't be able to fool Pandora completely, but my chameleon abilities did provide an advantage.

Pandora's beady eyes blinked at me as her gaze followed me into the forest. From the highest branch of the nearest tree, her view became distorted the moment I slipped between two trunks. My gaze darted upward to her position. She tilted her head to the side, then leaped into the air, spreading her own vast wings and reminding me that her raven was not small.

Several car engines came to life. I turned, swishing my horned tail to avoid the trees, and watched as the remaining staff drove out of sight. Now, it was only us.

I trudged under the canopy, dodging the shorter trees with a duck of my head and pushing gently through the branches. The trees had been my sanctuary as a child, and I would do everything I could to keep my flames away from them.

Pandora's scent invaded my nose, and I lifted my head and found her directly in front of me. She swooped down and flew past my right wing, then blew around my neck and back behind me. I backed up in surprise, realizing she wasn't the same slow and hesitant flier I had left all those years ago.

I launched upward, darting around the branches and away from Pandora. I wanted to be the pursuer, not the chased. My wings grazed a tree's bark as I swerved around its stout trunk and launched into the darker area of the forest, and then quickly veered off to the right and dove back toward the ground. My agile dragon body allowed me to move with ease, switching up my flying patterns at a moment's notice.

I threw a backward glance over my shoulder. Pandora had vanished.

A narrow passage of branches formed in front of me, and I folded my wings in against my sides to pass through to the other side. The little sunlight remaining illuminated the next section, and Pandora shot past me only a few yards away.

Realizing I was now behind her, I followed her as she soared back and forth in front of me. She searched for an opportunity to throw me, but I stayed close, weaving through the branches of the forest. We burst into the open sky, and the rush of the cooler wind against my face sent chills thundering across my larger body.

Pandora dove downward. I pivoted and followed her back into the forest, welcoming the warm embrace of the shadows. But then she shot through another narrow passage of branches.

To avoid tearing the vegetation, I sucked in a quick breath and pulled in my wings so tight, they shook. The trees shifted their branches away from me, and I released my held breath, nearly igniting a fire when sparks erupted into the air. I growled, watching Pandora's ease of flying. She flowed like the air itself, graceful and calm.

Pandora swerved to the left and disappeared onto a dark path. I slowed, lowering myself to the ground, and skidded against the dirt and rocks until I fully stopped. I ducked under the branches and peered around the tree trunks, searching the unlit area for her black feathers. I prowled forward, bent low to the ground to avoid breaking any branches, and peered deep into the thick of the forest, but Pandora had vanished.

Her scent had dissipated into the sky. I blew out a long breath. Her games were exhausting, and I didn't have time to play them. I turned toward the estate.

"Got you!" Pandora shouted. Her human form jumped out from behind a nearby tree, and she wrapped her arms around one of my legs.

Something sharp pierced the tender flesh between my scales.

I reared back, but Pandora held on to me as if glued. I stumbled backward, flicking my leg to throw her, and only managed to fall to my side. I chomped my teeth together and turned my neck to see Pandora better. She lifted her middle finger at me, then leaped to the ground and raced back into the forest, holding something in her hands.

A throaty roar of fire escaped my mouth, and I quickly turned to face the sky, fueled by rage. Once the inferno had cooled in my throat, I lifted my leg to examine the damage she had done, but nothing appeared out of the ordinary. It didn't make sense. But then again, this was Pandora I was dealing with.

I crawled backward, keeping my eye on the direction she had run, suspecting she had returned to her raven form. This had become a game to her, and I was her prey.

She was playing Ryker's game, the one that pitted us against one another and had us avoiding each other for days afterward.

The memories bit at the back of my mind. She really hated me, and I suspected this animosity had come long before I had escaped these lands. I had to put an end to this once and for all.

I leaped into the sky. My breath came in sharply as fury clenched at my chest. I navigated over the trees, searching for my sister.

Had she injected me with something?

An eerie quiet had overcome the forest. The sounds of the forest creatures and insects were silent, and the wind had stilled, leaving the air stale and thick. Even the trees' humming had muted to the point I could no longer trust my flying rhythm.

I swooped around a few circles, checking the pathways for any signs of life, especially my sister's. The forest remained still. From the corner of my eye, I caught several shadows slinking along the edge of the forest. I flew closer, but they dispersed like a dark fog, disappearing entirely when I flew directly over.

Fear pricked along the base of my skull. Nothing felt right.

I turned my attention to the estate and swerved toward

it. The inside lights had dimmed, and the sun had set completely, bathing me in darkness while I waited for the moon to rise. I peered upward at the stars.

A wave of nausea ravaged my stomach, and I folded into myself from the pain, landing near the front of the house on my side. I skidded against the rocky path, crying out as it tore at my scales, and came to a sudden stop. I collapsed against the ground and trembled from the pain radiating through my body.

Fear built inside me, crashing through me like a volcanic avalanche. I rolled to a standing position, panic taking hold of my mind, and another roar ripped from me, releasing the overpowering, consuming energy of dread. A tunnel of flames tore from my throat, igniting the estate like it was fresh kindling.

I stared in horror as the blaze spread like wildfire.

No.

I shoved my demon back to the recesses of my mind and shrank into my human form. My legs shook uncontrollably, and I collapsed back to the ground, staring at the growing inferno.

Thoughts of finding Mom and Mimi's charred bodies ravaged my mind. I leaped to my feet and teetered to one side when a wave of dizziness swept over me. I steadied myself, blinking several times to gain my bearings, then rushed into the estate. Despite my shaking legs, I tore up the stairs, fear pressing me forward with each step.

When I reached Mimi's room, I found Mom standing next to the bed. Mimi sat on the edge of the mattress.

She shook her head. "You should have never returned."

Her words gutted me, but I shoved away my hurt feelings.

Mom gave me a quick glance. "Paislee, what have you done?" she asked breathlessly.

The color in her cheeks had paled, but her eyes blazed with fury. She was weak, but her adrenaline would push her to safety, and that was all I needed from her for now.

"We need to go to the forest. You'll be safe there." I hooked Mimi's arm over my shoulders. "Come on. I'll explain later."

After making it down the stairs, Mimi slipped out from underneath us and pushed Mom and me away from her. "I'm fine. God, this family. I should have put a stop to all this years ago."

"And how would you have done that, Mother?" Mom clawed her fingers through her hair, pulling strands of it out at the roots. "This all started because of your choice to hide me from the king. Ryker would have never had control of us if you hadn't trusted him with our lives. He took everything from us. Everything."

I froze, half because of the information being revealed and the half because flames were nipping at the front door.

"We can have this argument outside," I said, grabbing Mom's arm and tugging her forward.

Mimi slapped her chest. "I told you I had Ryker under my control, but you had to go round up the others."

"He ruined my name! He threatened my children!" Mom screamed, shaking off my hold. She took several steps backward away from the front door, the color in her face draining to a shade of gray. "I needed the other fairies to banish him. Instead, you protected him, and we have been stuck in this hellhole since."

I stormed at Mom, desperation ravaging my insides. "Fight outside," I growled, latching my arm around her waist. I dragged her out the door with the fire licking our sides.

I dropped her to the first step, then whirled around toward Mimi right behind us. "Let's go," I snapped and pointed toward the forest.

Mimi nodded and circled me. I picked up my hoodie from the landing and slipped it back on, then followed Mom and Mimi. The silence between them was stifling, but I preferred it right now. I needed to think, and the space between us increased as I backtracked over the last hour in my mind.

Pandora had baited me into a fight. But then she hid until she could stick me with something. I should have been more attuned to her devious ways and found another way to end our fight. I didn't feel right in my body, but the more energy I expelled, the better I felt. Panic attacks were not normal for me, but this had to be one, because the thought of my sister actually poisoning me would kill me before it did.

My gaze darted to Mom and Mimi as they stepped under the trees' canopy. To my right, a shadowy figure shifted into view. I stopped dead in my tracks. I slowly turned, expecting to find Pandora, but instead, the man from the elevator stood a few feet away, staring longingly after Mom and Mimi.

EIGHTEEN

Pandora

A victory leap had me bursting from the forest before Paislee realized what had happened. I landed on my toes and twirled in a circle, then raced inside the house, flipping off the entry lights. I took the stairs three at a time and breathlessly burst inside my room.

Mission accomplished. Excitement surged through me.

I gathered the three other vials of blood and set them next to my bag. My black jeans and tank top slipped on easily, followed by my black jacket and boots. On the way out the back door, I dropped my runaway bag on the side of the outside stairs and headed for the garden.

That had been too easy. The Velcro spell had worked wonders. A few specific words muttered under my breath and Paislee hadn't been able to leave my grasp until the vial had filled with her blood.

I skipped down the dimly lit sidewalk and into the garden, admiring the tall willows that stooped to greet me with their slender, arching branches. Flowers had bloomed sporadically around the foliage, brightening the landscape in every direction with the help of the garden solar lighting and the lanterns evenly spaced along the path. Throughout my life, I had found solace and peace under the branches of these trees, and tonight those feelings would be renewed.

I had avoided this area since discovering what lurked below, and I missed my giant friends. My fingers grazed the bark of the nearest branch. Its hum filled me with joy. I would miss this the most.

The large vent nearest to the far end of the garden caught my eye. It opened to the underground tunnels and led to where Ryker and his men were waiting to be freed. I dropped to my knees in front of it.

The rusting grates had recently been wiped free of dirt and grime, and the brush around the vent had grown inward, cloaking some of it with branches. Mom had created the portal here, never thinking Ryker would find it if he couldn't venture above ground. But by mere accident, I had found a way to access the portal from this end. A quiet afternoon below the willow tree, me practicing my spells, had allowed Ryker to speak to me.

Mom's warnings had kept me silent that first day as I'd listened to his pleading. But the next morning I returned, ready to hear his side of the story.

Ryker's voice had coaxed me closer that day, and when he'd presented me with a chance for freedom, I hadn't hesitated. Paislee in exchange for never setting my feet on these grounds again. Sign me the fuck up.

A loud rumble bellowed above me, and a flash of light brightened the sky. My gaze shot upward and found fire licking the edges of the house.

Paislee's angry tantrums were going to burn down the estate. I let out a dry chuckle, more breath than sound.

Her flames crackled from the front end of the estate, but it was quickly spreading. I scrunched my nose from the smoke filtering into the garden.

I groaned. This was going to put a kink in my plans. I needed to move fast.

The stone bowl Ryker had instructed me to use clattered to the ground when I pulled it from my bag. I poured the vials of blood into it. With my pointer finger, I stirred seven times one way and another seven times the other way.

"Unbind, unwind, release the in-between that lies within these property boundaries." I said the words slowly, ensuring I recited it exactly the way Ryker had instructed. "Return what has been stolen and replace what once was, rewinding each step until all recent trespasses are undone."

I repeated it as I stirred, seven times clockwise and seven times counterclockwise. Rinse and repeat seven times.

Then I dipped my fingers and thumb into the blood and flicked it over the grates, circling them until all the blood had dripped into the tunnels.

Then I repeated. "Unbind, unwind, release the in-between that lies within these property boundaries. Return what has been stolen and replace what once was, rewinding each step until all recent trespasses are undone."

A circle of light illuminated around the grates, growing brighter with each passing second. I stepped backward. The light flickered, then flashed so bright, it blinded me. I winced and quickly turned away as a burst of air shot from the grates, and the light radiated like a high car beam, flooding the garden from one end to the other.

I looked up at the growing flames and tapped my foot impatiently against the dirt.

"Any day now, Ryker," I whispered under my breath.

I hadn't asked him how long it would take for the spell to release him—a detail I regretted not knowing as the flames spread and the light from the grates began to burn my skin.

A red-hued smoke seeped from the grate, startling me from my watch on the fire. I jumped away as the smoke slid across the ground, wisps of it slithering like a snake. I searched for a place to escape it, but it was either the fire, the burning light, or the smoke.

"None of those options are appealing." I glanced upward and dropped the bowl, hearing it clatter against the rocks. "I can leave now. No one said I had to—"

A figure from the other side of the garden caught my attention. I squinted at it. His focus was pinned on me, and he beckoned to me. I recognized Ryker's proud stance, with his chest puffed out and his shoulders rolled back. I blew out an exasperated breath.

"Just in the nick of time." I wrapped my jacket tighter around me and trudged toward the man.

Ryker's usual posse stood behind him, armed with guns and dressed in military garb. Their broad shoulders and oversized biceps reminded me of the fear I'd experienced as a child, having those overly brute men towering above me. But now, they paid me no attention as I approached Ryker. Beyond the ten normal guards, dozens of other large figures waited.

Where had they come from?

"Pandora." Ryker gathered my hands within his and kissed the tops of them. "I knew you had it in you. You always were my favorite." He winked at me.

I rolled my eyes and pulled my hands away. "Charming, but so unnecessary. Who are the goons?" I gestured toward the crowd of men.

Ryker folded his arms over his chest. "No one for you to worry about, love. Where is your mother?"

"In the house." I waved my hand in the forest's direction. "Or hiding in the trees. I can't imagine my hero of a sister would have left Mom and Mimi in the house to burn."

He closed the distance between us and cupped my chin in his hand. "Pandora. My sweet, sweet child. You know I cannot go into the forest. Please fetch them for me. If you don't—" He jerked his head toward the growing crowd behind him. "I'll send in the faceless ones in after them, and it won't be pleasant for those they find. And that goes double for those traitorous trees."

NINETEEN

Paislee

My gaze shot between the man and Mom. "You know my mom? Mimi?"

He looked my way and nodded. He pointed at his head where the curved, black horns protruded. "They are my people. You are too."

A chill ran down my spine. "You're speaking clearly again. Who are you?" I took one small step toward him.

He watched with a hint of amusement. "I've been following you for years."

My flesh prickled from his implications, and I frowned at him. "That's creepy."

"Someone had to keep an eye on you, besides your lover." The man faded slightly. He shook his hands in front of him as if it would help. "I don't have much time. Did you find the bottle at the back of Ryker's cabinet?"

"No. And it's a little late for that." I waved at the burning estate. "Is there another way to stop her from dying?"

His quick glance at the inferno showed little concern. "Why did you return here? I warned you to pick your next steps wisely." He interlaced his fingers and rested his hands against his abdomen, curiosity piercing me from his stare.

"Because my sister told me Mimi was ill, and I wanted to say good-bye." I looked around at our surroundings and found we were completely alone. "Who are you?"

"Like Ryker, I have been banished to an in-between, but I have not been bound to one place like he has." He faded more, but not before I noticed the twitch of a wing behind him.

"But I saw you so clearly in the elevator, and you spoke to me in the parking garage. The in-between prohibits that." I folded my arms over my chest. "You say we are your people. What are we? Mom and Mimi have only revealed we are cursed. And that Ryker did it."

"You're curious. I understand." He nodded toward the house. "Ryker will be here soon. The in-between does not hold if those involved do not stay in the places they should. The break in our reality, that allowed you to escape these lands, triggered the opening for me to follow, but it wasn't until the day in the elevator that you finally noticed me." His form faded to a shadow. "Maybe the day you decided to return home was when Ryker discovered

146

he could escape as well."

"Are you saying this is all my fault?" I hurried toward him, but his form blurred, then dissipated entirely. "Don't go. Please."

"I'll return as soon—" His voice faded without completing the sentence.

I blew out a frustrated breath and turned in a slow circle. The fire had burned out with only a few flickers from the roof lighting up the sky. My flame had not been hot enough, or a protection had been placed on the estate. As much as I hated this home, maybe it was for the best.

Through the scattering smoke, a shadow moved along the side of the estate. I squinted. The figure stepped into view and sauntered slowly toward me, with several other figures behind him. I knew that walk well. It was one I had tried to push from my memory for years. The confidence. His arrogance. It oozed off him like molasses, thick, sticky, and putrid.

Ryker. A sob rose in my throat, but I fought back the tears, determined to keep my wits intact.

His mouth curved into a wicked smile, and he held his arms out toward me. "Pumpkin. How I have missed you."

I rubbed my forearms, grimacing from my hated childhood nickname.

Behind him, a familiar figure stepped into the light.

Pandora.

An angry tear escaped down my cheek. "Why am I not surprised? You really are a traitor," I cried, unable to hold back my rage.

Heat rose up my neck, and without even thinking about it, my energy expanded, and I welcomed back my demon. I swished my tail, pivoting to strike Ryker, but he had already maneuvered out of the way, and I struck the edge of the estate instead. Pieces of cement and stones sprayed in every direction.

The smile on Ryker's face widened as he danced farther from my reach. His quick movements blurred together as if he were anticipating my decisions before I made them.

I turned to Pandora. A muscle in her jaw twitched, and with a puff of black smoke, a massive raven stood in her place. Pandora launched into the air, flying above my neck, then circled around my left side. Before I had a chance to react, she swooped toward my face with an ear-splitting scream.

I ducked, but not before Pandora's beak punctured my scales near my ears. I roared and spread my wings, knocking several men to their backs. I released my breath at them, igniting anyone I could reach. The fire rose again, catching on the charred bricks of the estate and lighting up the night sky.

I beat my wings and lifted from the ground, searching the sky for Pandora, but she had vanished again. Bitterness filled my heart. I felt myself slipping between caring too much about this family and giving up on them entirely.

I flew over the estate, checking the gardens and roof eaves, then turned my attention to the forest. I should have known. She had gone in to find Mom and Mimi for Ryker.

My lips curled back in a snarl, and I rounded back to find Ryker. He waved at me from the ground, a lopsided grin and an expression of confidence plastered on his face, that claimed I could not touch him. Fury thundered through me, choking me within its tight grasp.

Mom had told Mimi that she had wanted him dead at one time. That was enough to motivate me to complete the job.

The flames shot from my throat. He bounded out of the way with a laugh, my fire missing him by mere feet. But even with the proximity, the fire did not faze him.

"Do you really believe you can kill me, pumpkin?" Ryker asked, leaning against a nearby tree and picking at his nails as if he were bored. "I haven't survived this long to be taken out by one of the young ones. Even the elder fairies haven't discovered a way to end me."

I landed roughly, digging my claws into the ground to slow me down. The well-manicured lawn lay in shambles beneath me and embedded between my toes.

I roared again, turning my fire onto his estate. My flames covered the entire front, igniting it for the third time after the fire had dwindled once again. Anger burned hot within me, but underneath it was a cold, gnawing fear.

What if I couldn't stop him?

Several more guards stalked into view. I staggered backward, putting some distance between us as I searched for a way to end this battle before it became a war I could not win. One guard lifted a gun and pointed it at me.

"It's time to surrender." Ryker swept his blond waves out of his face and peered up at me.

One side of his face appeared wrinkled and obese from his chin to cheekbone. I blinked at the changes fading in and out. He shrank several feet, then stretched back to his six-and-a-half feet tall.

Shit. SHIT. What was that? My brain must be making this up.

I took another step backward, then braced against a large boulder.

Ryker's hand drifted to his cheek, and his eyes widened to saucers when his fingers touched a large lesion. He quickly turned that side of his face away from

150

me. "Return to your human form and call your family to meet with us. It's time we brought this family back together."

If this wasn't in my head, maybe it was a weakness of his. Which meant... This was my moment to strike.

I leaped at him, sweeping to the left and whirling my wing at him. Ryker toppled backward and fell on his back, hitting the ground at high speed. He skidded across the rocks like a rolling ball. My spirits soared from the surprised look on his face.

If I could speak, I'd let out a solid *fuck you*.

The sound of gunfire ripped my attention away from Ryker, but before I could respond, pain rippled through my left side. I shrieked. The fire in my throat blew out with the scream, and I turned it on the men, but not before another shot grazed my cheek. The searing burn radiated down my neck. I recoiled, taking several hurried steps backward before launching into the air again.

Their flesh burned beneath me, stinking up the air. The estate burned brighter, and the flames were spreading across the highest peaks. I circled to the backside of the building and ignited it from that angle, wanting more than anything to see Ryker's home burned to ash. Mom and Mimi could start over somewhere else. We did not need anything from this wretched man.

When I returned to the front, I found Ryker trudging toward the forest with dozens of men behind him. Where did they keep coming from?

I searched the landscape. A steady stream of men flowed from the side of the estate and down the hill toward the fields. A chill ran down my spine when I finally noticed their lack of features. The men had no faces. It was a long line of yes men, who would do whatever Ryker commanded, and they were headed toward me and my family.

TWENTY

Pandora

I swooped through the tree branches, looking for Mom and Mimi.

Ryker's words thundered in my mind. *"Please fetch them for me. If you don't, I'll send in the faceless ones after them, and it won't be as pleasant for those they find. And that goes double for those traitorous trees."*

I had never wanted anyone to be hurt. Damn Paislee. Why did she have to complicate everything in my life?

I stretched my wings wider, brushing against the tree trunks as I lowered to the ground. I cawed into the darkness, knowing Mom or Mimi would call for me if they were nearby.

Instead, a man strolled out from the unlit path. Jersey.

I flew past him, then circled back as his wings unfurled from his back and his horn appeared on his head. He raised a hand and waved at me. Jealousy ravaged my mind. Jersey slipped into his true form as effortlessly as a breath of wind. But I, chained to this human version of myself, could only summon one beast, a pale echo of the power sleeping in my blood. It was better to walk away than watch the flame burn in another's grasp.

Had he shown Paislee his newfound identity yet? Had he revealed the truth about who we really were and why we were trapped in these limited shifting bodies?

I doubted it. Everyone shielded her from heartache—especially him.

I croaked at him, "Liar." Then shifted to my human form several feet from where he stood. His brows lifted as I rose to my feet.

"Why have you come?" I asked, flicking my hair behind me.

His gaze softened, but he stared at me with the intensity of a hawk. "We could have found another way. You know this. I have told you this for years now."

"And as always, I remain entrapped while you roam free. I don't think you ever wanted to free us. Controlling, just like Ryker." I circled him, slinking like a lioness ready to spring on her prey.

He turned with me, his brows drawing together, uncertainty shadowing his face. "It was never going to be as easy as you wanted it to be. Our people are trapped as well."

"You have lied for far too long." I sprang forward and

then stood up straight, mere inches from him.

To my disappointment, he did not flinch or step away.

He leaned in closer, nearly touching his nose to mine. "I have disclosed what I know. Don't forget, I had no idea who I was either, so don't pin these lies on me. The deceit hangs on Ryker, and you know this. But still, you chose him over your own people."

Rage crashed violently against my skull from his last sentence and sent blinding heat thundering through every inch of my body. I narrowed my eyes and pinned him with my glare. "I chose me." My chest heaved with each furious breath, my heart pounding like a war drum against my ribs.

"Because you're selfish." He wiped at the perspiration beading on his forehead with the back of his arm. "Do you think this is just about you and Paislee? How many others will suffer because of your choices?"

"I. Don't. Care." I leaned back and held my finger like a gun at him, pretending to shoot. "Go save her. I have a hunt to complete." I whipped around and raced into the darkness.

I leaped into the air and shifted into my raven form, sweeping between each branch with exaggerated acrobats. Mom and Mimi were out here somewhere. I had heard everyone's excuses and reasons, but this time it was about me.

The moon's light streamed through the breaks in the trees, guiding me along the trail. The smashed leaves and footprints along the path caught my eye, and I flew above the path until it came to an end. I cawed deep and throaty, wanting my cries to carry as far as possible.

A rustle in the brush had me circling back toward it.

"Pandora," Mom whispered.

Mom stepped out into the path, pushing some branches out of her way. Mimi stood several feet behind her with tree branches wrapped closely, protecting her on all angles. The trees trusted me, but if they found out I had betrayed my family, they could possibly turn on me.

They had most likely overheard my argument with Jersey, which meant I had little time to coax Mom from the forest.

I hopped along the dirt and stopped a few feet from them, then transformed to my human form. The trees remained still, but I kept a watchful eye on them as I approached.

She bounded forward and wrapped me in her arms. "Are you okay? What happened?"

"Paislee and I were fighting. That's all. You can come back now." I patted Mom's back, then pulled away. "Everyone is fine."

"But the house was on fire." Mimi circled Mom and eyed me with clear disdain.

I shrugged, toying with a lock of my hair. "It must have not been strong enough. It's already out." A cold wind lifted my hair away from my shoulders, and I shivered from the assault on my senses.

Mom pulled off her sweater and threw it over my shoulders. "Where's Paislee?"

Anger surged, and my vision blurred at the edges. I nudged her away. "You're smothering me. Let's go home. I'm tired." I stomped onto the trail and threw a glance at them over my shoulder. "Are you coming?"

Mom slowly nodded. "Yes. Is Paislee safe?"

"Yes, Mom. Paislee is always fine." I beckoned them, then pulled the sweater snugly around me. It took every ounce of restraint not to pick up a rock and throw it at her. I hated all of them for forcing me to do this to them. "Come on, Mimi. We don't want you falling again."

A stream of fire lit up the night sky. I clenched my hands into fists. *Perfect*. Paislee always knew how to ruin a good time.

Mimi stopped short, then inhaled sharply through her nose, like she was sniffing out the truth. "You're lying."

I shouldn't have confined her to her room. The chances of her believing me anymore had become slim.

I rolled my shoulders back. "Fine. Paislee needs our help. Are you coming or not?"

"Why are you lying?" Mom asked. Her legs visibly shook as she hurried past me, then held her arm out to force me to look at her. "Who is Paislee fighting?"

"You set him free, didn't you?" Mimi asked from behind me, her voice coated with ice.

Mom drew in a long breath as she examined my face. "Please say no." She pressed the heel of her palms against her temples. "You didn't? Dora, please tell me you didn't release him."

A shadow flew overhead. I stole a glance just in time to see Paislee's tail. I dropped the sweater to my feet and gave Mom one last look as the remaining color drained from her cheeks. Somewhere deep inside me, I wanted to take it all back—to have never heard Ryker's voice that day in the garden and to have forgiven Paislee for leaving me. My chin quivered with the guilt rising in my chest.

"I'm sorry, Mom." I shoved the shame away. This was their fault.

I shifted and launched into the air, flying above Mom and Mimi and cawing harshly at them.

Paislee circled back around. I flew at her, aiming for her eyes, anything to hurt her and leave a scar. I might be the physically weaker sister, but I would win the battle of endurance. I spiraled toward her, pulling my wings tight against my body and using the wind stream to push me faster. Paislee noticed me in the last second and twisted away. I flexed my claws and rammed them into the side of her face, digging past her scales and penetrating the tender flesh near her ear.

She roared and threw her head back, trying to shake me away from her. I held on, digging my talons farther and relishing in the blood streaming over them. Paislee croaked, and small flames burned from her nostrils.

She plummeted toward the ground, taking out tree branches, and hit the dirt with a thud. She skidded and bounced, striking against a tree trunk and then another, nearly pulling it up by the roots as she finally came to a stop.

I flexed my claws, then released her and hopped to the nearest branch. Paislee shifted back to human form, clutching her head near her hair. Crimson rivulets flowed between her fingers and down her arm and face. Her gaze snapped to mine.

"You did this for nothing," she whispered, rolling to her side and hoisting herself to her feet. "He will never allow you to leave. And the faceless men who will tear this forest down will be the last thing you will see before Ryker entraps you for good."

I tilted my head at her and cawed. "Liar." What did she know anyway?

I climbed farther up the tree to surround myself with the branches' shadows, a perfect spot to watch my sister's ending as long as the trees did not revolt against me.

Mom pushed her way through the thick brush and half limped, half jogged when she noticed Paislee.

"What happened?" Her fingers trailed the side of Paislee's face, wiping at the blood.

Paislee flinched, but she didn't move as Mom wiped and smeared the crimson mess.

"It's nothing." Paislee winced and glared in my direction. "I'll live."

"Maybe you'll live." Mom shook her head as she peeled blood-soaked strands of hair off Paislee's cheek. "But if Ryker gets a hold of you, I don't know if I'll be able to save you. I'm not strong enough anymore. I drained most of my magic to keep Ryker locked away."

I suppressed a shudder. Did I hear her right?

"Is that the real reason to why you are dying?" Paislee asked, climbing to her feet and wrapping her arm around Mom to steady her.

"It's okay to die," Mom replied, resting her head against the side of Paislee's uninjured cheek. "We all die eventually."

"Not you. Not Mimi." Paislee wiped more blood out of her ear. "We're different. Magical. Ryker claims you're the villain out in the human world." She waved her hand erratically at the sky. "But in here, you're our mom. And you're not supposed to die."

"I wish I could tell you, baby. If only the contract hadn't—"

An explosion near the estate rippled through the trees, sending waves of energy crashing past us. Mom leaped backward and held onto the nearest tree to stabilize herself, while Paislee remained glued to her spot on the ground. Her gaze darted upward to me and then toward the estate.

I launched into the air and circled above the trees. Flames licked the night sky, and smoke filled the space around the estate, cloaking it from view. But I sensed the devastation and knew the trees were the ones suffering.

Deep shame grabbed hold of me, weighing me down with heavy guilt, and pulled me back toward the vegetation. My mind flooded with the trees' agony.

TWENTY-ONE

Paislee

"Maaaaalefiiiii!" Ryker bellowed from beyond the forest.

The inferno behind him spread across his estate, crackling and exploding as the pressure built.

The heat from my breath betrayed me, and I inched farther into the shadows of the forest. Mom stood as still as a statue several feet away from me, glaring in the direction Ryker's voice had traveled.

My skin itched, and the flames in my throat burned the words that I desperately wanted to say. I couldn't take back the destruction I had caused, but maybe I could give Mom a fighting chance to live out her last days in peace.

I had dozens of questions about the ghost and the nugget of information she claimed she could never disclose, but Ryker, his men, and the fire were too distracting to have this conversation now.

"I made you, Lefi. You and those spiteful daughters of yours. If I can ruin you once, I can do it again." His voice grew nearer as his men sawed at the trees, bringing them down one by one.

Their destruction ripped at my heart, and even the sky hung heavy against the trees' sorrows, as if the heavens mourned with them.

"I will destroy this forest if you force my hand." Ryker's voice carried, booming along the dirt ground like an earthquake.

I braced myself against the nearest tree.

"History does not have to repeat itself. I can always rebuild, but only if you surrender. All of you."

I felt Pandora's gaze burning into the top of my skull. I glanced up and found her peering down at me from one of the higher branches. Her feathers bristled and she turned her back toward me. The trees were her safety net, and after the years I had abandoned her, I didn't blame her for hating me. My heart knew this, but the blood caked on the side of my face prevented me from forgiving her.

Not to mention this was her fault.

Every inch of my body pulsed in agony. The fight to keep him away from them was relentless, and I would pay for it later. I didn't know if I could continue, but I had to find a way. I examined my arms and legs, surprised there wasn't more damage and equally disgusted by the filth. Dirt balls were embedded in my black locks, matting the strands together into a tangled bloody mess that would take days to comb through.

Tears flooded my eyes. The faceless men were closing in on us, the vegetation ached with their destruction, and all I could think about was my bruised body and messy hair.

My cheeks burned, and an inferno warmed my chest. I had to finish this—face the monster who was determined to see our downfall.

"Paislee." Mom's shaky voice pulled me from my thoughts.

I turned to face her, wiping my hand under my nose.

She shook her head slowly, kneading the heel of her palm against her temple. "Don't. Please don't go back there."

The exhaustion in her eyes broke me.

"You won't go back, Mom." I pressed my fists against my closed eyes. "I have to finish what I started. He can't have you."

"He always wins." Mom's hands circled my shoulders, and she leaned close to my ear. "This is my fate, to be his until the end of time. He clipped my wings long ago, and there is no going back."

"No," I snapped at her as I threw my arms to my sides. "No! I am not allowing this. I still have my wings. Same with Pandora. If she will stop her ridiculous vendetta against me, we can win this fight."

"Maybe, but he will win the war." She held up her hands and walked toward Ryker's voice.

"Mom, no!" I cried, then slapped my hands over my mouth, terrified Ryker would find us. The fire stirred in my belly, and the world began to spin. "You can't return, Mom."

She glanced over her shoulder at me, then her gaze drifted past me. "This isn't all Pandora's fault. Mimi will explain. She trusted a creature and all because he promised to save me from something I hadn't done. It was a setup to control my power. I'm sorry, my love, but I can't let this continue."

My gaze shot to meet Mimi's. "What is she talking about?"

I heard Mom's fading footsteps and turned back toward her. "Mom, stop. Just wait, for hell's sake." I jogged to meet her.

Pandora landed on a branch near Mom and shook her feathers as if she disagreed with me stopping Mom.

"You were once powerful, Mom." I grabbed her arm to stop her from leaving again. "You have this chance to end his hold on you. Why won't you stand with me against him?"

"I told you." She wrapped her hand around mine that held her and pulled it away.

"Because he clipped your wings? You don't need to fly. We need your fire. You need to prove to yourself that he cannot put his foot on your neck ever again." I circled in front of her, hugging myself tightly across my chest. "Please stop running toward him. Don't let him take anything more from this family."

"You don't understand, Pais," Mom whispered in a hoarse, cracked tone, as if the effort to speak was painful. "I used it up. That's why I'm dying, and there's nothing—"

"Malefi!" Ryker yelled, his voice much closer this time.

"How can he be this close?" I whirled around, searching the darkness for his men. "The trees won't let him in."

"You know this is for the best!" he hollered, his voice coming from another direction.

I leaped to the side, expecting to see him through the trees, but he wasn't anywhere to be seen.

"He's projecting his voice," Mimi said as she limped in between me and Mom. "His illusions are growing stronger, which means he has tapped into your energy again. This is nonsense. He will kill you. Let's return home and end this charade."

"Wait. Illusions?" I scowled at Mimi. "Has he always used illusions?"

Mimi's brows raised, and she shot Mom a sideways glance. "It can't be explained any more than that." She grabbed Mom's hand and pulled her down the path. "We are returning. You have no idea who you're messing with."

"Then tell me!" I screamed, frustration biting at the back of my skull.

"It's not possible." Mimi waved, but did not turn to face me.

"Who is the tall man with the long, dark hair and horns protruding from his head?" I asked, placing my hand on Mimi's shoulder as she walked past me.

Mimi froze, but she did not turn my way. "Lefi, did you tell Paislee? Is that why Ryker escaped so easily?"

"Malefi, if I find you first, I will do to your daughters what I did to you!" Ryker sounded farther away and in an entirely different direction.

His games were grating on my last nerve. As if sensing my fury, the nearest trees leaned in closer, covering us with their branches. I leaned into their protection and expected Mom and Mimi to do the same, but they moved out of the way.

"No," Mom replied to Mimi. She pushed the branches to clear a path to me, then wrapped her arms around me and squeezed. "If you're seeing them, then it's only a matter of time before Ryker realizes it. Clear that man from your mind." Her hands trembled as they grazed my arms. She stepped away from me.

"Who are they?" I grabbed her hand to stop her from leaving but looked at Mimi. "Tell me."

"We can't." Mimi closed her eyes and pinched the bridge of her nose. "Please don't ask again."

I bit the inside of my cheek to keep myself from snapping. "You can't or you won't?"

"Both." Mom pulled her hand free from mine and walked away without another glance. "This is how it has to be. For you. For Pandora. For me and Mimi. And definitely for the tall man you saw. They are safer without us in their lives." She disappeared into the darkest area of the forest, leaving me with nothing but hopelessness filling my heart.

TWENTY-TWO

Pandora

I watched Mom leave. Paislee wrapped her arms around herself, rocking gently in silence.

Guilt flooded over me, but I quickly smothered it. I knew who that man was and why Mom and Mimi couldn't tell Paislee. But I could. If Jersey hadn't told her, then maybe it was best she suffered by not knowing the truth of our origins.

Another explosion ripped open the night sky, and I rocked on the branch I stood on as the waves rushed past me. Pain wrenched my mind. The trees were suffering, and I needed to put a stop to it.

I spread my wings and swooped near my sister and Mimi, cawing at them with disgust. My claws dug into another branch, and I steadied myself just ahead of Mom. I croaked a cry, driving into her the urgency of her arrival. I did not understand Ryker's obsession with Mom, and I hated myself for not caring, but if Mom had just been honest with me from the beginning, maybe we wouldn't be in this situation.

I couldn't see past the mistakes Mom had made, and I knew it was wrong to not try. She deserved to be heard and understood, but my mind refused to give her the benefit of the doubt.

The moon had set, and the darkest time of the night settled in. The soft wind carried whispers of a life I had never known, and I struggled to remember a moment of true joy that would melt away the bitterness consuming my thoughts.

We made our way through the forest with the fire's light guiding the way.

Mom walked with her head held high, despite stumbling on occasion and having to use the trees' support to continue down the path. Her weakened body rebelled against her determination to end this battle.

Mimi followed several yards behind, but Paislee had disappeared again.

My nerves prickled with each passing second, feeling like pins along my skin.

The fire from the estate barely flickered as we left the trees canopy, but the disaster at the edge of the forest was what brought Mom to her knees. Pieces of several ancient trees lay strewn across the property, leaving gaping holes where their roots had once stretched deep into the earth.

I cried with Mom, landing near her and picking my way through the rubble. The agony ripped at my heart.

Ryker waited patiently near the front porch, and his men dispersed to the edges of the forest, standing with their backs toward us in militant form. The faceless men marched in the direction of the underground tunnels, but instead of entering, they veered into the fields. Their shadows stilled, and they blended with the night's colors.

I transformed into my human form. When the black smoke dissipated around me, I noticed Mimi nearby, but Paislee was not with her. Mimi's eyes narrowed at me, then she pursed her lips and gave me a quick nod.

Ryker appeared before me.

His fingers trailed down my cheek. "Your eyes." With his thumb, he pressed against the tender skin below my eye. "What happened in the forest?"

"I fought Paislee and won this time. That's all." I didn't dare to shake away his firm grip on my face, but it hurt. I took a step backward, and his hand fell away. "I brought them to you. I've held up my end of the deal."

He chuckled with a tilted shake of his head. "Something has changed, my love." His hand snapped forward, and he grabbed my arm and yanked me close to him. "I'm not done with you, especially now."

"You can't have her!" Mom leaped forward, shoving

him with all her strength.

He stood like a brick wall and never took his eyes off me. "I don't need you anymore, Lefi." He shoved her back.

She staggered backward and hit the ground with such force that she slid several feet along the rocky path.

I stared at Mom in horror as Mimi ran past me and crouched next to Mom.

"You stupid woman," Ryker hissed, reeling me closer against him. He pinned Mom with his glare. "You thought you were clever, banishing me to the in-between. Little did you know, you put me exactly in the place that allowed me access to find Paislee."

Mom choked on a sob, her eyes widening to saucers as tears gathered in them. Mimi embraced Mom tightly, her arms circling her waist, while Mom leaned against her, resting her head against Mimi's chest with a weary tenderness.

"That's right. You abandoned me in the very portal that showed me where to find your precious daughter. I only needed someone in this reality to connect with hers." He slid his arm around the front of my chest and patted my shoulder. "It didn't take much to convince your naughty child to go along with my plan."

"No," I whispered. A deep ache hollowed me out as I

realized what I had done. He had used me to not only escape but to tear apart my family. And I had been so desperate to punish Paislee and leave this prison, I hadn't questioned it.

"It's okay, my love." His lips grazed my ear. "I will provide a good life for you. All you have to do is submit."

I forced down a sick feeling. "You told me they would be safe," I whispered, straining against his hold on me.

He tightened his grip. "And you believed me. That's the best part of this entire show." He trailed a finger down my cheek and along my collarbone. "You are so innocent, but a full-grown woman now. Any bloodline of your grandmother's is fresh for my picking when they are no longer a child. You belong to me now."

I recoiled, but he yanked me back to him.

Terror seized every muscle in my body. "Ryker, no. Please. I did what you asked."

"Your pleas sound so familiar. Just like your mother's." His hand cupped my chin, turning my face to see him.

Flecks of black swirled in the blues of his eyes, mesmerizing me. My thoughts splintered, struggling to process his meaning. I blinked and swayed to one side, gripping onto Ryker's arm to stabilize myself. A strangled gasp escaped my lips. Mom and Mimi had both stood here with Ryker, faced with desperation, and now I understood everything.

A smile blossomed on Ryker's face. "Good girl. Do you want to make a deal with me as well?"

"Don't listen to him, Dora!" Mom yelled, her voice shaking with weakness. "He will take everything from you. Drain you until you don't recognize yourself."

"I will immortalize you," Ryker whispered, his eyes pulling me in further. "You will never die, and we can be together forever."

His words made no sense. Why would I ever want to be with him forever?

"Let her go!" Jersey hollered.

Jersey's voice pulled me from Ryker's trance. I blinked several times, then tore my gaze from Ryker and found Jersey standing over Mom and Mimi. Ryker's men circled us, training their guns on Jersey.

"Don't mind him," Ryker said, wrapping his arm around my shoulders. "It will all be over soon."

Dark horns adorned Jersey's head. I rubbed my eyes and stared at Mom and Mimi. Both had horns protruding from their heads, and Mimi's dark wings had expanded.

"Your illusion is faltering, Ryker," Mimi said as she climbed to her feet. "You can't keep a hold on us any longer."

Ryker squeezed me tighter and yanked me toward the house. "I don't need much time, Esther. You know this." He snapped his fingers at his men. "Hold them. I'll return shortly to handle their punishment."

I dug my heels in, but he pulled me alongside him.

"I don't want this, Ryker. I want to leave, just like we agreed." I squirmed against his hold.

His gaze darted to mine, and a dry chuckle slipped from his lips. "You betrayed your family. You absolutely chose this." His arms circled my waist, then he heaved me up and threw me over his shoulder.

I screamed and tried to transform to my raven, but nothing happened. I slammed my fists into Ryker's back and kicked my feet, doing anything I could to destabilize him, but his grip on my legs only tightened.

"No!" I cried, swiveling my torso to see Mom. "I'm sorry, Mom. I didn't know. I just wanted to be normal."

Tears flooded Mom's face as she wept. "It's not your fault, baby. It was never your fault. Only mine." Her body sagged forward, and she hung her head, sobs shaking her entire body. "I'm so sorry, my love. I would give anything to take back that day." She gripped her knees and rocked back and forth, her cries growing louder by the second.

I wanted to look away. I didn't. I couldn't. Watching her break felt like a betrayal, but not watching felt worse.

175

My heart ached for what I had done and the choices I had made to bring this moment to fruition.

"Shut her up," Ryker barked as he stomped toward the estate.

His men closed in on her. One of them lifted his arm and brought it down fast and hard, striking Mom on the side of her face with the butt of his gun. She grunted and tumbled to her side. Mimi cried out and crawled toward her. Another guard held a gun to Jersey's head.

I grabbed my hair and my scream tore free, raw and savage, echoing with a terror I didn't know I could feel.

TWENTY-THREE

Paislee

A dark fog swept in when Pandora screamed. I stared from the safety of the forest as the scene unfolded so quickly, it was difficult to register. Panic and utter confusion paralyzed me. The horns on Jersey's head had been startling, but when they appeared on Mom and Mimi, I had to rub my eyes to make sure I wasn't hallucinating.

They were identical to the ghost who was stalking me.

But Pandora's scream brought me reeling from my disbelief.

My aching joints and bloody face were no longer a concern as my transformation into a dragon ripped branches from the trees and tossed them yards into the air. I expanded my wings and roared, blowing flames toward the estate. I emerged from the forest, knocking over the nearest guard and crushing him under my feet.

His final cry was cut short when I twisted my leg that held him to the dirt.

Ryker stopped short and whipped around, his greedy gaze landing on me. A grin pulled at the edges of his mouth, and he winked at me.

If it was the last thing I did, I would ensure Ryker never smiled again.

My nostrils flared as I stormed toward them. His men scattered, leaving my family and Jersey to fend for themselves. Guns fired, and I flipped my left wing out, ramming it into three men and throwing them against the stones of the estate with bone-jarring thuds. The sound of their bones breaking fueled my rage, and a low growl rumbled up my throat.

When I faced the estate again, I found Ryker dragging Pandora kicking and screaming toward the front door. Her teeth locked onto his wrist, and she clenched with so much force, his pained howls echoed across the valley. He knocked her away and grabbed his arm, a surprised expression permeating his features.

He hadn't expected to be hurt. I tilted my head, trying to remember a moment when Ryker had expressed pain. But not a moment in my memory revealed a time that he had shown any weakness.

I lunged forward, taking the opportunity to strike. I swung my tail in his direction but stopped short when he tilted his head to look at me. His face had distorted, and festering lesions were spread across his cheeks and chin. Where once had been a full head of hair, baldness with short wisps of hair peppered around the ears. The person in front of me looked nothing like Ryker.

As I stared, he lifted his hand to touch his face. Darkness clouded his features, and Mom's shrieks filled the space between us. I wrenched back from the noise as another sound of marching feet invaded my ears.

Jersey scooped Mom into his arms and raced for the forest. My gaze darted from my family to Ryker, as I tried to make sense of his features, when a realization struck me like a bag of stones to my gut. I gasped.

The illusions. Ryker wasn't human.

He straightened his posture, and his facial features blurred, returning to his normal appearance. He shook his injured arm from Pandora's bite and lifted it with a smile, showing me he had already healed.

I growled. How?

The missing seven men circled the side of the estate, holding a large weapon between two of them that was locked onto me.

Ryker held out his hand toward them. "Paislee, I have you and your family surrounded."

I glanced at each side, discovering the faceless men had encircled us. Mom slid from Jersey's arms and leaned against him, watching as the guards closed in on them. A deep rage burst like a bomb inside me. I reared back, then stomped onto the ground, sending a thundering vibration across the land. Several men fell like bowling pins, but most stood their ground, including those who had the weapon aimed at me.

A guard fired a warning shot that burned past my ear.

Ryker wobbled but danced in a circle and steadied himself. His smirk resurfaced. "You won't win. If you surrender, I will ensure your mom and grandmother are treated well. I only want you and your sister."

My gaze turned to meet Pandora's. She was trembling so hard, her teeth chattered. Mom had moved away from Jersey and held Pandora against her. The faceless men hovered feet behind him.

Mimi gave me a slight shake of her head and mouthed, *Don't do it.*

From behind her, a tall man with horns on his head came into focus, shimmering against the dark landscape but illuminated by the lights from the house. My eyes widened as the shimmer grew, and more horned people came into view. My gaze swept across the property. They were everywhere, holding weapons and preparing to fight, their attention pinned on Ryker.

Hope surged within me. Ryker was outnumbered.

My flames licked my throat. I opened my mouth and let out an ear-piercing sonic screech, followed by a long breath of fire directed at Ryker's men. I leaped to the side and landed with a thud as the weapon fired and its shot blew past me. I swerved to the other side, then pummeled into Ryker, sending him flying into the half-circle window above the doorway.

He grunted and tumbled to the ground. The glass cracked, spider veins traveling in every which direction.

Battle cries grew with intensity, and I didn't have to look to know my people were fighting Ryker's men.

I lumbered forward and wrapped my teeth around his leg, then clenched my mouth shut.

His screams warmed my heart. I tossed him into the air, noting the utter surprise and terror in his expression as he spiraled through the air and crashed heavily to the rocky ground. When he cried out in pain and grabbed at his right shoulder, the skin on his face wrinkled, and the same lesions scattered across his chin.

"Paislee!" Jersey bellowed, a warning vibrating in his tone.

I ducked, but the blast struck my side, rolling me backward at an exceptional speed. The world spun above me, disorienting my vision and causing vomit to worm its way up my throat. My shoulder screamed in pain when it hit something hard and unmoving, followed by a torturous agony radiating from my injured side.

My guts wrenched and expelled everything left in my stomach as I sank into my human form. I curled within myself, coughing uncontrollably and gasping for breath at the same time. My esophagus burned, and the throbbing from my side stole all my attention.

Screams and yelling registered in my mind, coming from the direction I had been. I pried open my tear-filled eyes and blinked at the smoke and flurry of figures entangled with one another.

I rolled to my knees and pressed my palms to the dirt. A fog edged its way into my sight, and I fought the urge to vomit again as I tilted to one side. I caught myself on my elbow and blinked repeatedly until my eyes focused.

The forest loomed a few yards away, and I half crawled, half wormed toward the safety of the trees' protection. I didn't know if I was dying or simply so injured that I could not focus. With each movement, I swayed to one side, and the forest blurred to the point I thought I would pass out.

I squeezed my eyes shut and continued crawling, using my hands to guide me through the rocks and sticks lining my path. My focus remained on putting distance between me and the battle.

The shouts grew with intensity, and I could no longer differentiate the voices entangled in the fight. I feared my family had perished but could not bring myself to look as I sensed my life draining from my body. I exhaled, then inhaled. My palms snagged on rocks and twigs with each inch toward the forest. Exhale. Inhale. My knees pushed me forward. Exhale. Inhale. The wetness traveled across my chest and to my neck.

Exhale. Inhale.

The air cooled around me, and silence stretched on for far too long. I felt the coarse texture of a branch wrap around my torso. I exhaled a long, relieved breath and relaxed into the protection of the tree.

TWENTY-FOUR

Pandora

A deep-throated scream ripped from my lips when Paislee struck the large stone on the far side of the driveway. Her body wrenched, and her limbs blew out in every direction. Mom's arms shook within my hold, and she nearly collapsed to the ground. I wrapped her close and held tight, watching Jersey sprint out of my view.

The scene exploded with movement. Dozens of new people were around us, with horns adorning their heads. I blinked at them in confusion, trying to register where they had come from and how I had missed them.

"I'm sorry, Dora," Mom whispered. Her legs gave out beneath her, and she pulled us to the ground.

I settled on the dirt with her, never taking my arms from her torso. "I'm sorry too." Sobs bubbled in my throat. I couldn't fight them back any longer.

"We didn't think he could get to you." Mom's fingers combed through my hair, and she kissed my forehead. "He cursed us so long ago that I hadn't remembered his power could be extended once your powers fully manifested. I should have protected you better."

"My powers?" I pulled back to see Mom's face. Dirt and blood were caked down the sides of her face, and for the first time, I could see the agony and regret laced in her expression.

Mom cupped my chin. "Your eyes. They are glowing, bright and green, just like mine had many years ago. You have stepped into your full powers, and he can now use you like he did me."

I rubbed my eyes, doubting her words even though I had seen the hungry way Ryker looked at me.

"I know we are dark fairies, Mom. Jersey told me." We hadn't had the luxury of time to fully discuss it, but at least I had a name for my ability to change form. Not that I ever believed we were human. I kneaded my knuckle into the corner of my eye to squash the burn from the smoke and grime. "But what do you mean by my powers? Are you talking about magic? What did Ryker do to you?"

She grabbed my hand and pulled it upward. "You have been united with our family. Feel your head."

I palmed my forehead and slid my hand into my hair, widening my eyes when I felt a hardness sweep upward, then curve forward again, ending in a spike.

My gaze darted around the fighting scene surrounding

us, and I stared in shock at the dozens of people protecting us from Ryker and his men. Mimi stood tall above us, watching with curious interest. Wings jutted out from her back that had not been there before, but her horns faded in and out as if a thin veil covered them.

"I don't understand." I turned back toward Mom. Clearly there was more to dark fairies and their community than I'd realized. "How were all of these people kept from me and Paislee?"

"We couldn't speak of it. If we did, the curse extended to you and Paislee, regardless of your—" A crimson flush rose into Mom's cheeks, and a coughing fit overcame her. She scooted a few inches backward, terror overtaking her features as she pointed behind me. "Please run, Dora. Do not allow that man to take you inside the estate."

I glanced over my shoulder and saw Ryker sauntering through the fight as if it did not exist, his gaze locked onto me.

"He's pulling what is left from me, baby. And he will drain you the same way. Run," she croaked out, falling onto her back. She held her hand toward me.

I crawled to her and pulled her head into my lap. "I can't win against him. How do I stop him from killing you?"

"He holds an elixir in his room that he has hidden. I

cannot venture into his sitting room, so I suspect it's in there." Her fingers wrapped tightly around my wrists, and she peered up at me. "But, baby girl, you and Pandora are the daughters of the high dark fairies. We come from royalty and possess the most potent magic. What she can do, you can do. And vice versa. He has kept you small for a reason. Go now. Find your sister and defeat him."

Her hold on me loosened as her eyes closed. Mimi fell to her knees beside me.

"Go now." She pushed at me and took Mom's head from my lap. "He's closing in, Pandora. You have to run. Do not allow him to do to you and Paislee what he did to your mom and me."

"Mom!" I cried, shaking her shoulders.

She didn't respond, and her body swayed back and forth with each thrust.

Mimi shoved me harder. "You must go. This will be your fate if he captures you."

I focused on my shift, and a dark fog suddenly surrounded me as my wings unfurled and I leaped into the air. Ryker stared up at me. Recognition flashed through my mind. His features melted into a stranger's face, which resembled the boggart painting hanging in his sitting room above his fireplace.

I flapped my wings toward the stars, noticing a

difference in my wind speed and strength. I turned my head toward my wings and nearly tumbled back to the earth when scales came into view instead of my usual feathers. A heat warmed my throat, and a burst of elation rushed through my heart.

What she can do, you can do.

Mom's words echoed in my head. All these years of envying Paislee, and the power had already lain dormant within me. Mom and Mimi had never said it out loud, but there had been hints I had not heard. Their babbling lectures that had made no sense suddenly unraveled in their truth.

Ryker had played with us all, and I had heard him above everyone else's warnings. And now my sister would pay the ultimate price because of my choices.

My joy plummeted from the horror of my actions. Years of planning had been nothing but a naive girl's revenge tactic. I had been safe from Ryker because of Mom's sacrifice, and instead of thanking her, I had freed him to destroy us all.

I circled the forest, searching for Paislee and keeping a close eye on what was unfolding near the estate. Ryker had to be stopped, and I needed my sister's help to end it once and for all.

TWENTY-FIVE

Paislee

Blood mixed with vomit and snot dripped down my cheeks. I wiped it away with the back of my filthy arm, smearing dirt across my face. It was useless, and it didn't matter.

I stared through the branches and up at the sky. A large shadow flew by, but it resembled my own form, when I transformed. I had to be in a nightmare of my own making. Or death was knocking, and hallucinations had set in. Either way, my time was coming to an end.

The trek to the forest had felt like years had passed, but once I had made it to its safety, the exposed tree roots had scooted me along. Between the branches and roots, I had made it far enough into their cocoon that I could barely hear the battle any longer.

Maybe I would die here, but at least I would be surrounded by love.

Every inch of my body radiated with utter pain. I didn't want to budge in fear an unknown injury would reveal itself. Whatever had been shot at me had damaged my side to the point I did not believe I would recover. Every time I lifted my hand from that area, fresh blood dripped between my fingers. I had lost too much to recover.

I thought I heard my name called several times, but no one came for me. The voice must have been in my head, along with the dragon figure circling above me.

I blinked as the trees and sky ebbed between faded and focused. My ears were clogged, and I tasted a rancid metal on my tongue. It didn't seem like I had long to wait, as more shadows were dancing in my peripheral vision. Maybe the ghost that had been haunting me had come to take me away.

"Pais." A man's frantic voice stirred at my thoughts.

Soft fabric folded over my chest, and I sighed from the comfort it brought me.

"I have you," Jersey whispered.

I yawned to clear my half-clogged ears, but my hearing didn't get any better. Jersey's face came into view, then blurred again. I clung to his shirt, desperate to keep him with me until I passed over.

"You're healing, Paislee." His fingers tried to comb through my hair but caught on the knots and grime.

I winced.

His hand came back to my face, and he lightly brushed my cheeks and nose. "I'm so sorry. Give your body time to catch up. You'll be good as new soon."

I choked up a laugh. What was he talking about? My end was consuming me.

My leg shifted, and I heard a crack before white-hot agony lanced through my side like lightning in a storm. A scream filled the space around me, but then I realized I was the one making the noise. I clamped my mouth shut. Another blinding pain shot up my leg, radiating into my core. My body bucked upward, and every muscle in my body tightened.

Then relief spread as if morphine had been injected into my veins. The relaxation had me inhaling a slow and deliberate breath. A smile tugged on my lips, and I blinked at the tree branches above as they swayed with the wind.

Pandora. Ryker. I bolted upright and looked every which way. Jersey rubbed his hand on my back.

"I'm alive?" I pinched my arm. My eyes widened as I stared at him. "Oh my God, I'm alive!"

"You healed yourself." Jersey pulled my hair over my shoulders and wrapped his jacket around them.

"What about my mom? Pandora? Mimi?" I climbed to my feet and stared suspiciously at the horns adorning his head. "Did they stop Ryker?"

His lips pressed into a straight line, and he shook his head.

"For fuck's sake." I dropped his jacket and yanked my demon's power to the forefront of my mind, but nothing happened.

"Give it a minute." He held out his jacket to me again. "We can walk back to the estate."

I brushed past his outstretched hand, refusing the offer without a word. "There's no time," I snapped, my voice cutting through the trees like a knife. I flicked a hand toward the curling horns now crowning his brow. "And when did you become that?"

I didn't wait for an answer. The forest swallowed me as I broke into a run, leaves and branches whipping at my face. I couldn't afford a creature lesson now.

But I heard him behind me.

The shadow I had seen earlier flew above again. I skidded to a halt and searched through the branches, but whatever it was had already disappeared.

"Pandora." Jersey stopped beside me. "She's the one in the sky."

"She made it then?" I hugged my torso tightly.

"I think so, but she isn't what she used to be." He pointed upward. "She looks a lot like you now."

A surge of electricity shot through me, and my breath

hitched in my throat. I bounced on my toes across the dirt ground, shocked by the sensations traveling through my limbs. A curdled yelp bubbled up my throat. I grabbed a tree trunk and steadied myself before examining my arms and legs.

"Paislee!" Jersey exclaimed, chasing after me. His brows shot up, almost disappearing in his hairline. "Your eyes They... Holy shit, they are glowing like embers."

I touched my eyelids, but a terrified shriek stole my attention. My demon burst from me without thought, and I transformed as I leaped into the air. I maneuvered through the branches and crashed into the night sky seconds later.

Another dragon circled above the estate. I darted toward her, knowing it was Pandora. Her roar vibrated across the valley, followed by a steady flame that lit up the entire sky.

When I reached the fight, Pandora had landed. Her gaze darted to mine. Near her, Mom lay on the ground, unmoving, with Mimi and several horned people surrounding her.

My body seized on me with tremors jolting through my limbs, and I hit the ground with a thundering impact. I slid across the gravel road, taking out faceless men with my wings and tail. When I screeched to a halt, I turned and faced those who had hurt my family. Ryker's arms folded over his chest, while his gaze shifted between me and Pandora.

I released everything I had inside me, lighting up the estate and the men protecting Ryker.

TWENTY-SIX

Pandora

Ryker strolled from the flames, unharmed from Paislee's inferno. He watched the chaos unfold with a detached sort of glee, as if he knew something no one else knew. The horned people protecting Mimi's and Mom's bodies flickered as he drew nearer, then disappeared completely.

"This is my property," he hollered, pinning me with his stare. "My rules. My law. My fucking illusion."

A shimmer of light streamed between him and Mom, so light and breezy I almost missed it. He was still siphoning her energy when she barely had any to offer—draining her beautiful and giving essence—and I had been oblivious to it my entire life. She wasn't dead, but he was damn sure ensuring her end if I didn't stop him now.

Shame curled through my insides, wrenching at my heart with such force, my body shrank to my human form. I tumbled to my knees next to Mom and Mimi.

"That's right," Ryker said, sauntering closer with two

of his men flanking his sides.

Did he ever run out of them?

"I will end her now if you do not bend to my will." He rubbed his palms together, then snapped his fingers in my direction. "Take her inside."

My gaze darted to Paislee, who was fighting off dozens of Ryker's faceless men. They were rising from the earth like cockroaches. When one fell, another replaced him.

We were here because of me. I had no choice but to surrender. I owed my family that much after my betrayal. I lifted my hands and nodded.

The men dragged me to my feet.

"No!" Mimi cried, lunging toward Ryker.

He turned on her and grabbed her by the neck, then lifted her off the ground. Mimi swung at him, striking him in the arm repeatedly as her legs flailed beneath her. He smirked, his brows lifting with clear amusement.

His form flickered, and I blinked several times at the grotesque creature standing in his place. A boggart. Lesions swarmed his face, neck, and hands, his wrinkles so deep, there were other sores peeking from the folds.

His illusion.

My blood ran ice cold. Had we really been prisoners in Ryker's illusion? All these years? Even with the evidence in front of my eyes, my mind could not wrap around the deceit. Had my entire world been a lie?

Mimi's arms fell to her sides, and a purple hue spread into her crimson cheeks as her face contorted in twisted pain.

There was a roaring in my ears, like the world had gone underwater. Mimi fighting for her life, Mom motionless on the ground, and Paislee overrun by a swarm of clones, every second moved at a snail's pace. All I could focus on was Mimi's life slowly draining from her.

I yanked at the men's hold on my arms, straining so hard my skin tore under their grip. "Let her go, Ryker. You have me."

A smile stretched on his wrinkled and distorted face. He didn't look my way but slowly lowered Mimi to the ground. She collapsed, gasping in a breath, and the purple hue in her lips disappeared.

"Mimi!" I screamed, pulling so hard my shoulders felt like they would dislocate.

Ryker waved a dismissive hand in my direction, and his men hauled me away. His insidious laughter echoed against my back, chilling me to the bone.

Why hadn't Mom told me? Why had Mimi allowed this to happen?

It didn't matter any longer.

We stepped onto the stairs leading to the front door. I strained to see Paislee, but she had moved to the side of the estate, wrestling with the hordes of militant clones. Her fire lighting up the sky and an occasional roar were the only indications that she remained alive.

Ryker's men dropped me inside the foyer like a sack of potatoes. I fell to my hands and knees, staring at the stone floor that I had walked across hours earlier on my pursuit of freedom. This had been a sham, a con… a manipulation to drain power from Mom so he could live in a fantasy world of his own making.

Everything I had been fed had been lies.

I crawled to my feet, exhaustion seeping into every inch of my body. Ryker had returned to his normal-looking self, but it was easy to see the mask he wore: a disgusting, old goblin who used powerful women to obtain a lavish lifestyle.

Ryker lifted his brows toward the staircase. "I will follow you to my suite."

"And what will happen there?" I asked, inching away from his men.

"Don't be a fool, my love." He chuckled and gestured toward the staircase again. "We are beyond negotiations. Do not make this harder than it has to be."

I bolted up the stairs, taking the steps three at a time

for the second time today and ignoring the pain in my chest as I reached the third floor. I sucked in a lungful of air before racing down the corridor and bursting through Ryker's suite doors.

I had to find the elixir before he arrived.

The lights flickered when I snapped them on, and I half expected Paislee's ghost to emerge, but the room remained quiet. I tore toward the bar, shoving the bottles we had left on the floor out of my way as I dove at the cabinets. There were dozens of bottles remaining in the back of the cupboard.

I pushed the obvious ones aside, straining toward the back and feeling around. Each bottle I pulled out had a liquor label on it. Bottles clanged together, rolling away from me as I flung them out of the way. I stretched as far as I could and finally touched the wall. My fingers closed around a small, pear-shaped glass. Footsteps behind me had my heart thrashing against my ribs.

I pulled the bottle out and turned it over in my hand. The lid was long and pointed, suctioning to the inside of the bottle's neck. It lacked a label and had no markings anywhere on it. This had to be it.

I shoved it into my pocket and rolled to my knees as Ryker's men walked into the room. They flanked the entrance and then Ryker appeared between them.

His gaze drifted across the strewn bottles, and a smirk lifted the left side of his lips. "What did you find, my little pet?"

I slowly rose to my feet. "I want the truth, Ryker. My mom and grandmother. What did you do to them?"

He ran his fingers across the counter opposite me. "Exactly what your grandma asked me to do. Erase the damage your mother did."

"And what exactly was the damage she had done?" I spoke slowly, enunciating each word deliberately as I took a small step toward the nearest window, never taking my eyes off him.

"Oh, I wouldn't want to taint your mother's image." His chuckle was low and humorless, like he was savoring my pain. "Actually, I would love to do that, the ungrateful twat."

I flinched. How dare he speak about her that way?

"She could have had it all," he said, his voice low and curling like smoke. "Fame, fortune, the spoils of the highest bloodlines. Instead, she chose to have *you*... and your sister."

He studied me with eyes like dying embers, as if weighing if it was worth the breath it would take to snuff me out. "And by the terms in your grandmother's contract, inked in blood and shadow, you were protected until your eighteenth birthday."

A cruel laugh rasped from his throat as he turned away, gliding past the furniture in the room.

Chose, he said, like we'd been plucked from the gutters of the town on our mother's whim and raised by Ryker because he was a good person. I slid one foot, then the other, slow as a breeze, toward the fractured light of the window.

"I played her game. Mimi was useless after I drained her of her golden essence but unfortunately protected as well." He flicked at some lint on the back of the couch, then turned his attention back to me. "But your mom, she had plenty to give me and, damn, has it been a delight to relish in her energy." He jabbed his finger at me. "She is one powerful fairy. I could have lived off her magic for eons to come, but she had to ruin it all by binding me to the in-between and using most of her energy to trap me there."

And I took her protection and destroyed it, right before her eyes. Every memory from the past few months felt like a blade now, pressing just under my skin.

"Get to the point, Ryker." I slipped my hand in my pocket and ran my fingers along the bottle. I owed Mom this, a chance to survive my betrayal.

"Your mom played rough with some other fairies, and

the king himself had to get involved. By the time I arrived, the other fairies had accused your mother of poisoning the princess, and the entire kingdom was demanding your mom's head on a spike." He sank onto a nearby chair and crossed one leg over the other. "I put a stop to that nonsense and saved the day. And this is the thanks I received."

My heart sank when I noticed the locks on the window. It would take me precious seconds to release them, but once I was out on the ledge, Ryker wouldn't be able to reach me. I knew the ledge walk well, and if I was able to scale down the wall using the vine trellises, I could hide the bottle and shift to escape. Once I shook his men's tail on me, I would return for the elixir.

"You're telling me my grandma asked you to save her daughter by siphoning off magic and draining them both completely?" I threw up my arms in disbelief to hide my slide that brought me closer to the window. "Do I have that straight?"

He pursed his lips. "When you put it like that, it doesn't sound quite as heroic." He stood with a shake of his head. "No, my new little pet. I saved your mom from her choices, and in return, she gifted me a lifetime of magic to use as I please, for whatever I please." He waved his hand around the room. "This estate, your privileged lifestyle, our expensive taste are all because of your mom's gift to me."

His revelation gutted me. Mom had provided all that I had known, and Ryker was taking credit for it. "You're insane. Greedy. Selfish. You don't deserve to have a face of a man when you're only a spineless goblin."

His expression darkened, and a muscle in his neck twitched with his tightened jaw.

I grabbed the window locks and yanked them open, then thrust the glass upward. It stalled halfway. Terror knotted in my stomach, and I couldn't breathe. Not properly. My hands shook so badly, I could barely grip the lip of the window as I yanked desperately at it, but it did not budge.

Ryker's fingers snaked around my neck, and he squeezed. "Little naive pet," he whispered as his lips grazed the top of my ear. "Did you really believe escape would be that easy?"

TWENTY-SEVEN

Paislee

Pandora had been dragged into the estate without much of a fight. The faceless men had me pulled into the field, away from my family and unprotected by the trees.

The more men I lit on fire, the more streamed out of the underground tunnels. What deal, with what devil, had Ryker made?

I shook off the half-dozen men clawing at my legs, stomping them as I pushed my way back toward the estate. Another flood of men poured toward me, forcing me back again. I unfurled my wings, but several men jumped for them and held them down with their weight.

I roared again, shaking them loose, and set the field on fire. The flames erupted at some unseen chemical, blowing me farther away from the estate. I tumbled backward, curling into myself until I slid to a hard stop against the gathered rocks and dirt. When I looked up, a tiny hint of the sunrise gleamed at the eastern end of the sky.

We had been at it all night, and my muscles screamed for the fight to be over.

I rolled to my feet and shook off the dirt, pain radiating down every limb like thousands of daggers buried in my flesh. The men were recovering, and even with no eyes, they were searching the field as if they could see.

Despite my achy joints and my bruised muscles, I leaped into the sky, but exhaustion gripped my strength, and I careened back toward the field. I dug deep, finding little will to continue but somehow steadied myself, and darted directly over their heads. With dread in my heart, I watched them watch me.

The way they stared at me, unseeing but somehow sensing me, sent an eerie chill slipping down my spine, feather light and slow, as if fingers were tracing my vertebrae.

Ryker's army might not be able to die, but he would perish if it was the last thing I did.

I landed near the front stairs and slid to a bumpy stop close to Mimi and Mom. My chest heaved in and out as I gathered enough oxygen to fuel my muscles. It didn't help, so I had to shift back to my human form.

Mom remained wrapped in Mimi's arms and covered by a blue shawl that had not been there earlier. I stumbled toward them, wiping the relentless perspiration from my brow with the back of my arm.

"This is all my fault," Mimi said. Her shoulders sagged forward as if the weight of Mom and whatever secrets she held were dragging her to her deathbed. "Ryker had been my friend. I trusted him, but I shouldn't have."

"Who is he really?" I crouched next to her, grasping my trembling knees to steady them.

"It's too late." She lifted her chin to look at me, while gripping Mom's frail frame tighter. "He has Pandora. He will take what he needs from her and become unstoppable once again. Look at what he was still capable of doing with limited power." She jerked her head in the direction of the field.

I didn't need the reminder.

I trailed my finger down Mom's cheek, noticing how pale her skin had become. My only reassurance that she lived was the short gasps of breath she took, which surely would not provide the oxygen she needed to survive.

"I don't care what he has done. I need to prevent what he could do. Who is he?"

She flipped her hair out of her face. "His true form is grotesque, but he had a heart once upon a time."

I bit out my reply. "His heart is not my concern."

"You're right; it shouldn't be. His mischievous ways actually delighted the fairies and people alike, which was part of his charm and how I got roped into this mess from the beginning." A vacant gaze overtook her features, like the light inside had gone out. She nodded toward the house. "He's going to use your sister's essence to maintain his illusive life, and she will become his prisoner like your mom has been."

I furrowed my brows, processing the little information she had given me. "So who am I really fighting? A man? Or something else?"

She sighed. "He's a boggart, Pais. A goblin who has enchanted everyone by using your mother's magic. It's most likely too late, but if you can find a way to trap him again, she might have a chance."

I slowly rose to my feet, even with the approaching hoard of clones. "Was any of this real? Was my life outside of this place an illusion?"

"Go, Paislee." Mimi's gaze darted from me to the footsteps behind me. "They won't go inside."

"What about you?" I snuck a look over my shoulder to see the faceless men marching in a military form.

"They don't need me anymore. None of them will pay any attention to us." She pulled Mom closer to her. "Go, now."

Mom's eyes fluttered, but they didn't open. She was alive. Barely.

This was wrong, but I ran across the rocky path and dove over the threshold before the men reached me. They stopped short outside. I slammed the door in their faceless expressions.

Silence greeted me as I grasped the handrail and looked upward. The lights were on, but there was no movement.

I climbed with caution, checking every which way for Ryker's men or Ryker himself. Each floorboard that squeaked sent panic thundering through me, causing every muscle to tighten. I stepped as lightly as possible, avoiding steps I knew were loud. If I made it out of this alive, I would need the longest soak in the hottest bath.

The slow walk to Ryker's suite gnawed at my nerves. My skin itched with heat, and I wanted to shift to release the inferno inside my gut.

I heard voices when I rounded the corner that led to his suite. I inched closer, noticing one of my least favorite of his men covering the doorway with his back toward me. His broad shoulders and bulging muscles were nauseatingly big, and I knew I didn't stand a chance with him. I would be a ragdoll in his hands.

But he was slow, and I wasn't.

I crept toward him. His confidence in never looking around and only watching the other end of the hallway was unnerving. I continued regardless. If I died, it would be a better alternative than having Ryker drain me for years on end.

When I had closed the distance, I dove for the doorway, rolling over the threshold and into the entryway. He grunted, and I assumed he'd caught me because I launched into the air. Then I flapped my wings and shot upward.

I cried out, cawing with delight. In my peripheral vision, I noticed feathers instead of scales.

A croak of joy bubbled up my throat, and I swooped out of reach from another man as he jumped for me. My smaller raven frame allowed me more agility, so I soared to the ceiling and grazed the texture before turning into the sitting room.

Ryker stood at the other end of the room with Pandora in front of him and his fingers curled around her throat. His gaze locked with mine, and he squeezed Pandora's throat.

Pandora's eyes widened from the threat, revealing glowing, bright-green irises. Now I understood Jersey's words from the forest. Mine glowed red. We were something more than these demons we could shift into. And the horned people who had arrived to help us were connected to us. To this.

209

And this man, *this boggart*, holding my sister hostage had orchestrated a massive illusion, one I had escaped by chance. But unless the fabric of reality ripped open again, I could see no second opportunity. This had to end another way.

"You can't stop me, Paislee," he bellowed, holding up a glass bottle with his other hand. "Your mom will die without this. If you come closer, I will dump it on the floor."

I circled near the ceiling to stay out of arm's reach to his men. He popped off the lid to the bottle and tilted it. I cawed angrily at him, fury heaving at my chest as my vision blurred at the edges. Pandora pressed her lips into a straight line, digging her nails into Ryker's forearm as she side-eyed the bottle.

"What will it be?" One of his brows lifted, but the other drooped, revealing an oozing sore below it.

He was running out of time. Desperate and weak men would do anything to win. I could call his bluff, but Ryker had never been one to lose.

I flew to the other side of the room, opposite his men, and shifted to my human form. Ryker's men started toward me.

"Stop. I'm here to surrender." I held out my hand and turned toward Ryker. "Take me instead. Use my magic, not hers. She wanted to experience life outside, so let her, and I will stay with you."

"No, Pais." Pandora tried to shake her head, but Ryker held her firm.

His laughter echoed off the walls, hollow and cruel. Like a predator toying with prey, he said, "How heroic of you." He clicked his tongue. "But who said I only wanted one of you?"

"Greed looks ugly on you," I said, folding my arms over my chest. I had met men like him out in the real world. His arrogance would hate to know his true form had been revealed. "It's showing on your face."

His expression melted into a frown. "You lie."

"Ask your goons." I nodded toward the men. "Your senior years have not been too kind to you."

He released Pandora and shoved her behind him, then stuffed the lid back into place on the bottle. "Is it showing?" he asked the nearest man. He turned his face to one side and then the other.

The man shook his head. "She's lying."

"But somehow, I know you have lesions and gushy, wrinkled rolls down your cheeks. Meh." I shrugged, counting my breaths, each one a tether holding back the urge to strike. "Must be my imagination getting the best of me that your face droops so low, your eye sockets are exposed."

The exaggeration was a nice touch. Ryker's nostrils flared, and he stomped his foot like a petulant child. I choked back a fit of laughter. Who would have known his appearance would be the detail he treasured the most?

Pandora shot him a look over her shoulder, then slowly stepped away, holding her hand up in the air.

"Who are you? What have you done with Ryker?" A look of horror rose in her expression.

Pride surged inside my chest. She was a total bitch for baiting me here, but she knew when to listen to my cues.

A red hue spread over Ryker's face, and he stomped toward the guard. "*You* lied to me."

The guard backed away, holding up his hands. "It's only showing a little. I wouldn't lie to you, Ryker. She's messing with—"

Out of thin air, a sword appeared in Ryker's hand, and he thrust it through the man's throat, then drove it in, twisting it with a quick snap of his hand. What had the sword cost Mom?

I took a quick step backward, holding my hand out to Pandora. The man stuttered and gripped the sharp side of the sword before Ryker yanked it out. Blood oozed from the now-gaping hole as the man fell to his knees, then tipped to his side. His eyes blinked several times, and he pressed his hands against his throat, gasping for a breath that evaded him. Seconds later, his limbs relaxed, and his struggle ended.

Ryker turned his attention to me.

Pandora had inched closer to me but stopped in her tracks when she noticed Ryker turn our way.

His facial features had contorted and slumped even further, revealing a complete stranger with wisps of gray hair on a mostly balding head. His stubby hands and shorter stature surprised me, but his look of hatred did not.

"Your mom will perish for this moment." He picked up the glass bottle, which he had dropped onto the nearest chair, and lifted it for me to see. "You must see who I really am now, but you will quickly forget once I possess your power."

I held my arms in the air. "Give Pandora the bottle, and I will stay here with you."

"Good girl." The desperation in his expression was replaced with a look of satisfaction.

I nodded at Pandora. "Save Mom."

Pandora stood still, staring at me in disbelief. "He will drain you, Pais. You cannot give him what he demands." She waved her arm toward him. "Look at his disgusting features. He will require too much for you to handle."

"Stop talking about my appearance!" he bellowed,

white-knuckling the bottle to the point his arm was trembling.

"Don't underestimate my powers," I snapped at her, then walked her way. I gathered her hands in mine. "Go now. I am not saying good-bye to anyone today."

She shook her head, but I shoved her toward Ryker.

"Leave, Pandora. I no longer want to see your face after all your lies." I turned away from her.

Her sigh was all I heard. I stole a look over my shoulder to watch her walk toward Ryker. His glare turned into a smirk as she approached, but he held the bottle out to her. His other hand twitched with the sword.

Panic stole my breath. My feet tripped over each other when I whipped around, and I reached for my sister as I tumbled to my knees.

"Pandora," I cried, reaching out to her.

"One of you will do." Ryker slashed the sword across Pandora's chest.

Her shrieks filled the space, and I cried out to her as I crawled her way. Ryker tossed the bottle, and it hit the wall before crashing to the floor. I couldn't see if it broke, but I climbed to my feet anyway.

Ryker stood over my sister's crumpled frame and slammed the sword downward. The sound of metal breaking bone crawled up my skin, and my stomach revolted. I tried to scream, but Ryker's arms had already snaked around my throat, clamping any noise from escaping.

A burst of adrenaline jolted through me, and I jabbed my fingers into his eyes, then elbowed him in the chest. He screeched like a banshee, releasing his hold on me. I staggered backward, running into a warm body. A fresh wave of terror thundered through me, and a searing-hot blast of heat shot from my chest.

Before I could turn to see who was there, a flash of light brightened the room, sending streams of colors in every direction. A rainbow prism flooded every corner, shooting and swirling with a fury of energy. I lifted my trembling hands and found the colors streaming from them, connected with Pandora's fallen form.

The rainbow twirled like a tornado around Ryker, tightening around his flailing limbs and squeezing against his chest. His shocked expression plummeted into despair, and he wrenched forward, crying in pain. His eyes widened when he stood up straight again, then he bent backward as the colors contorted his body, twisting and turning until he crumbled into a ball on the floor.

I fell to my knees and crawled in the direction Pandora had fallen, covering her with my body as screams filled the air around me.

TWENTY-EIGHT

Pandora

The pain pressed suffocatingly at my chest, and the illumination in the room forced me to squeeze my eyes shut. The life draining out of my body occupied my thoughts, and I barely noticed when Paislee covered me with her body.

Humiliation coiled through me, even in my last moments. Ryker's sword had buried into my ribs, and my raspy and painful breaths warned me that my last one would arrive soon. I had brought this upon myself, and my ending fit the crime I had committed against my family.

But I didn't want to die, and I would give almost anything to have a second chance.

The pressure of Paislee lying on top of me suddenly entered my awareness, and I wanted to push her off, but strength evaded me. Angry and regretful tears gathered in my eyes. This strategy to obtain freedom had been for nothing. I would never know the smell of the ocean water or the sensation of digging my toes into the warm sand. Instead, I would die a traitor.

The weight on my body lifted, and the pressure in my side dissipated, followed with an intense pain radiating in my ribs.

I pried open my watery eyes when the light faded and found Paislee kneeling in front of me with her hand clamped over my side wound. It was no use. I wanted to tell her, but the words were stuck like glue in my throat. Even after all I had done, she wanted to save me.

"Don't die," she whispered, her voice quavering.

I tried to look at her but couldn't move much. Everything hurt. But behind Paislee, Ryker's unseeing eyes stared back at me. Any signs of life were gone, and at least I would die knowing his end came before mine. That small piece of knowledge warmed my heart.

"I shouldn't have stepped through the light without you," Paislee said. Her soft voice filled me with joy.

I didn't deserve her. My silent apology hung on my lips, fragile and trembling, like a moth near a flame.

"I wouldn't have left you on purpose. The light vanished; I promise it did. I wanted to come back for you and take you with me, but I forgot about you and Mom and Mimi so quickly." She paused, wiping a tear from my cheek. "And in the strangest way." She leaned closer to me, pressing harder. "Damn this blood. Please, stop."

Her sobs shook against my ribs.

I grunted from the pain. "How?" I managed to croak out. Some form of liquid dripped from my mouth.

Paislee's concerned and hopeful expression came into view. "I will heal you, Dora. Just hang on, please."

"How…" I croaked again. "Did. You. Forget." Each word took so much effort. I nearly passed out from the exertion.

She shook her head. "Don't speak." Then her eyes glossed over, staring through me instead of at me. "I don't know how I forgot. One minute the light had my full attention as I desperately tried to reach you, then it was gone. It felt like moments, but it probably wasn't… I found myself far away from home. I don't know how I arrived there or how long it took, but a new life unfolded for me in the most opportune ways. I remember you, Mom, and Mimi were here with Ryker, but at the time, I could not remember how to return, and the longer I stayed away, the less I wanted to come home. My fear turned into motivation to heal and grow, and I made peace with never seeing you again."

It had to have been Mom who'd made her forget. Her magical abilities could cross any portal, any timeline, and any reality, which was why Ryker had targeted her. Who else would be that motivated to keep Paislee from returning?

"I missed you, but I could not bring myself to think of you often, not until I arrived back home." Her gaze returned to mine. "I don't know why. It pains me to think I forgot so easily."

I lifted my hand to her bent knee, barely having the strength to hold my fingers on her. "I. Am. Sorry." I sputtered out the last word, coughing on the blood filling my throat.

"No!" Paislee cried, releasing my side and wiping at my mouth. "Don't speak. Please." She used her shirt to wipe my mouth clean of blood, but I knew there would be more soon.

"They're in here!" Jersey yelled from the other end of the room. He came into view and stared wide-eyed down at me as he held Mom's frail frame in his arms. "Where's the elixir?" His gaze never left mine, but he spoke to Paislee.

Paislee rose from her knees, and I heard one of them pop loudly, but she didn't complain or wince. She pulled herself to her feet and looked around, then pointed at the nearest wall.

"Over there, I think. It might have shattered."

Jersey laid Mom on the couch, and another man with

black horns appeared in my view.

"Give the elixir to her first," the man said, and he pointed at me.

Jersey lowered to his knees in front of me, and the strange man leaned down and shifted my head to stare at the ceiling.

"Open your mouth, Dora," Paislee said. She kneeled on the other side of me and gathered my hands into hers. "I won't leave you."

I did what she asked, and Jersey tipped the bottle enough for a few drops to fall. They landed on my tongue, and I closed my eyes as I swallowed hard, tasting the blood in my throat. I wanted to vomit but I fought the urge, giving the elixir time to penetrate whatever areas it could before it was too late.

It felt like too late had come and gone, but I wanted to believe I still had time to heal.

"My sister next," the man said, taking the bottle from Jersey.

Paislee shot a look in the man's direction. His sister? We had an uncle?

A sharp pain stabbed at my side and chest, and I wrenched upward from the sudden torment ravaging my insides. I gasped in a breath of beautiful, refreshing air, but the throb intensified. A scream tore up my throat, and

I curled into myself as Paislee rubbed my back.

"It will be over soon," she whispered in my ear.

Another scream sounded, but it wasn't mine. I pried my arms from my sides and glanced upward at Mom sitting straight up, her gaze darting around the room. Her attention fell on me and then Paislee before she leaped off the couch and threw herself at us.

I cried when her embrace squeezed my ribs, but the pain was subsiding. I melted against her. My sobs rose in quick breaths, and I heard the same from Paislee.

"My babies," Mom whispered in my ear. "I wanted to warn you. I wanted to save you from his hell, but my words were bound by his hold on me. I am so sorry. Will you ever forgive me?"

She rocked back and forth, squeezing us so tight, I could barely move, but I didn't want her to stop.

"Who are we?" Paislee asked after a few minutes of silence. She pulled back and looked at Mom.

I blinked at her in confusion and then pointed. "Paislee, your head. And eyes. And... what the actual fuck?" I sat up straight. "You have wings, but you haven't transformed into your demon."

Paislee's startled expression melted into laughter, and she pointed at me in return. "Look at yourself." Her other hand lifted to her head, and she ran her hands along her

221

black horns.

I crawled to my feet, but not before I saw the same features on Mom and everyone in the crowd that was growing inside the room. Mimi pushed through them, and a smile blossomed across her face. She clapped her hands together and intertwined her fingers as they touched her chin.

"You've done it. He must be dead." She rushed to my side and gathered me into an embrace. "We are free again, my love." She pulled back and looked me up and down. "You will finally have your freedom, more freedom than you could ever imagine."

TWENTY-NINE

Paislee

"But I don't understand," I said, interrupting the cheers of joy around me. "Who are all these people? Why do we have horns and wings? And for the love of the goddess, can someone please explain how my memories of this place were dulled while I was gone for ten years?"

That was the mystery that played repeatedly in my mind. I had wanted Pandora to be with me when I'd escaped, but then I suddenly hadn't cared either way. In fact, I had been relieved to no longer have the family burden on my shoulders.

Mimi kissed my forehead and pulled me in close to her and Pandora. "Let's have some tea in the sunroom, where you can see the true outside view."

Pandora's brows furrowed. "The true outside?"

"We were trapped inside Ryker's fantasy illusion." Mom leaned into our circle, wrapping her arms over mine and Pandora's shoulders. "We couldn't speak of it or speak of his true self or even hint to our situation to anyone. If we did, you two would no longer be protected through the age of eighteen. We had eighteen years to find a way to protect you."

A look of dread melted onto Pandora's face. "The curse to the in-between?"

Mom nodded. "I had been planning it for years. After Paislee escaped, I had to speed up my plans, and her being gone made it much easier to keep us all protected. Our division was a blessing, despite not feeling that way." She pressed her cheek to mine. "Even though I would have given up most anything to see you again. But not your safety. Not our safety."

"But who are all these people?" Pandora asked, waving her hand backward at the crowd. "Who are we?"

With eyes gleaming with unspoken pride, Mimi lifted her chest as her heart stood taller. "We are the fairies, my loves. The dark fairies. You think your transformation into your demons is powerful?" She clucked her tongue. "You are in for a real treat."

Jersey walked up to us, the horns on his head completely visible and wings jutting from his back. He jabbed his thumb over his shoulder. "There are a lot of our people waiting for a chance to speak with you four."

My gaze locked onto Ryker as his body rose from the floor, dragged upward by an unseen force. The veil that

224

had cloaked him had now unraveled, revealing the twisted and grotesque features of a boggart, skin like swamp-mucked leather and a face frozen in a sneer of malevolence that held too many secrets to count. The man I had known had been a phantom stitched together with lies and illusion. The truth stood before me and in its shadow, the life I had known cracked like bone. I could not fathom the depth of the deception, nor the hollowness it left behind.

"What will be done with him?"

Mom bumped shoulders with me as she turned to watch. "He will be burned on a pyre, and his ashes will be returned to the earth. This is the circle of life. Good or bad, we will all be sacrificed to Mother Earth again."

She slipped her hand in mine, and her other hand gripped Pandora's. We followed the crowd and left the room behind Ryker's body. I did not want to honor him, but I felt drawn to the traditions I hadn't been included in before.

"Your brother?" I pointed at the dark-haired man who had first appeared in the elevator.

Mom's gaze drifted toward the man. "Yes. He promised to watch over you two as best he could. I haven't seen him in over twenty-five years."

"What's his name?"

"Lysander." She smiled when the man turned our way. "We were best friends."

He stopped and allowed the few in front of us to pass by him, then he gathered Mom's hand in his and kissed it. "Maleficent. How I have missed you."

Mom rose to her toes and planted a kiss on his cheek. "And I have missed you. Thank you for watching over my baby."

His smile widened and he turned our way, falling into step next to me. "You two were infants the last time I saw you." He cast us a veiled glance. "Once Ryker's curse consumed the land, your presence was like an apparition, fading in and out, but never aware of us. We walked the same land but lived separate lives."

"We were your ghosts." Pandora shivered as she and I looked at each other. "That's creepy."

"And my room? Really?" I shot him a scowl.

He shrugged. "I'd never entered your room until that day. The estate stood dark with no way to light it from our end, but your room lit up the day you returned. My intentions were to capture your attention, not frighten you."

We reached the stairs, and several people transformed into hawks, eagles, and a variety of big cats. The birds swooped downward, while the cats moved with fluid grace and silent precision down the steps, each one returning to their fairy form at the front door. Pandora's eyes widened as she watched, then with a puff of her black smoke, an eagle flew after them.

Mom's face lit up with joy. "You can be anything you want, Paislee." She squeezed my shoulder. "After being confined for so long, your magic yearns for expansion. If you could choose any beast, what would it be?"

She circled me and walked toward the steps, glancing back at me as if expecting me to have already shifted. I had never thought of being anything but a dragon. The raven form had been foreign to me, but I hadn't disliked it. What would it be like to prowl the earth, instead of fly above it? The ideas were endless and intriguing.

I followed the crowd, mulling over all the options I now possessed. Pandora never hesitated. She thought about her actions after the fact, but not me. I had to think about my next steps, especially after recent events.

I reached the foyer and followed Mimi and Lysander outside. The morning sunrays stretched across the blue sky, lighting up the forest that had expanded around the estate. But within their canopy, dozens of home structures lay across the horizon. And the estate remained intact, absent of burn marks on the white stones from our nightlong battle.

A large fountain was in the middle of the grounds, with statues of fairies circling it. Flowers blossomed in every direction, and all types of fruit trees were scattered through the fields in between the homes. I stepped onto the green, lush grass and bounded on my toes from the energy of the earth beneath my feet.

It was like nothing I had felt before. A current of electricity sparked with each step, and instead of it draining me, energy streamed through my veins like molten lava.

Mom's gaze drifted skyward, the sun's light painting her face in a fleeting gold. She closed her eyes as if in surrender. A faint smile ghosted her lips as shadows gathered at her feet. A black fog coiled around her legs, slithering up her frame like a lover returning from the grave.

It did not just consume her, it awakened her.

Her form dissolved into shadow and scale, bone reshaping like cracking ice and seconds later, her beast emerged. Her wings, now regrown and healed, shimmered with dark fire as they spread with unnatural grace. She reared back, released a roar that shook the very marrow of the earth, and sprang into the sky with a fury born from long-forgotten freedom.

She rose above us until the clouds above swallowed

228

her whole.

"Isn't she marvelous?" Lysander stood next to me and folded his arms across his chest.

"Mom?" I gave him a curt nod. "I've seen her fly more times than I can count, but this time felt different."

"You've never had the opportunity to witness her real magic. I'm sure she is eager for you to find your own as well." He shielded his eyes with one hand and stared down at me. "You surprised me."

"Pardon." I rubbed my hands together, enjoying the sparking sensation between my palms.

"The day in the elevator... You had never noticed me before and then you looked right at me." His brows lifted with a soft smile. "You did something that day that changed everything. I knew if I could keep reaching you and you really decided to return home, I might have a chance to undo Ryker's hold on my family."

"But what did I do?"

"I suspect it was the choice to return that did it." He pointed toward the forest, a grin lifting his cheeks. "I followed you the day you launched yourself through the light. I knew I had to stay with you and make sure you were safe. But then your memories faded, and you found happiness with normal people. The mundane suited your nervous system."

"Did you stay with me the entire ten years?" I didn't like the sound of that, but a sense of gratitude for his protectiveness overcame me.

Affection glowed in his eyes when he turned to look at me. "Not always. You found some good places to land, with a little nudge from my side. Then I would leave you for a while, checking in from time to time. Your mom had secured her and my mother's and Pandora's safety." He patted my arm. "We had to live our lives the best we could as well. I really didn't have any hope in changing anything until that day in the elevator."

Jersey waved at me from beside the pyre that was being built. I nodded in reply. "Why didn't you tell me then?"

"Lysander," Mimi said, hooking her arm through his. "What do you think of my granddaughters?"

The corners of his eyes crinkled. "They are quite extraordinary. Who would have thought they would be the ones to break this curse?"

"They take after me." She patted his arm with her free hand. "Let's join our people."

He nodded before turning back toward me. "To answer your question, would you have believed me?"

I thought back to that day and how unsure I had been about everything, and I gave him a mirthless laugh.

230

"Probably not. But then later, you couldn't really speak to me."

Mimi shooed me forward.

"I'm going," I said, laughing for real this time and then dancing down the path when music reached my ears.

I didn't need Lysander to answer me. This place had been cursed. Communication had been dulled so extremely that I had been lucky to receive any at all. I wanted to be angry about what I had lost, but I had found freedom for ten years, while Pandora had never known it. Seeing her laughter and joy as she danced with the other fairies brought happiness to my heart that shone like a lighthouse in the dark.

Jersey pulled me close from behind and nuzzled my neck. "Do you find me less attractive now that you see who I really am?"

I turned around in his arms and pulled him closer. "Are you kidding me? A handsome fairy. I would be a fool to not be attracted to you."

He let out an unrestrained whoop of delight, then pressed his lips to mine. I melted against him, breathing in his scent and yearning for nothing more than to be alone with him. His tongue parted my lips and dived into my mouth, signaling he was feeling the same way.

I broke the kiss and licked my lips. "I want more of

that later."

"Deal." He planted a kiss on my forehead.

We turned to face the pyre, watching the flames grow around Ryker's body. My whole life I had been afraid of that man. Fear had been his way to control the women in his life. But come to find out, he had been nothing but a weak creature, draining my mother's unbound essence to give the illusion he was someone who mattered.

My gaze drifted around, taking in the new views and the hundreds of fairies. I had been given a second chance. Gratitude danced through my heart, and for the first time in my life, my spirits soared.

THIRTY

Pandora

The green grass squished between my toes, and I curled them in with joy fluttering through my chest. I stared at the estate. A colorful essence danced around the edges, playing with the sunshine and wind.

That had not been there before. Or if it had, Ryker had made sure we would not see it.

I had debated on staying, but after a few good nights' sleep and a long talk with Paislee, I wanted the opportunity to explore the human world like she had. Where she had been lacking because her magic hadn't fully manifested, mine was flourishing and would provide for me at a moment's notice.

No one knew how the fabric of reality had ripped open the day Paislee had escaped. The idea that she had manifested it out of desperation, tapping into a force unknown to the fairies, was a possibility most others had settled on. I found the idea intriguing and hoped to discover the truth once I left these lands.

Mimi opened the front door and walked toward me, shielding her eyes from the sun with her hand.

"Was it always this beautiful to you?" I asked, pointing at the sparkle of color filling the air.

She stopped and tilted her head upward. "Before Ryker stabbed me in the back, yes. There was nothing but peace in these lands." Her gaze shifted to mine, and she lowered her hand to her side. "His desire for fame and fortune caused him to destroy everything wonderful in my world. It's unfortunate, because he was once a great friend."

"I hate that he turned on you when you trusted him." I held my hand against my chest, thinking of the deceit my life had been built on. "How does anyone obtain safe relationships?"

Her fingers traced down the side of my face, and she brushed a wisp of hair behind my ear. "When you find out that mystery, make sure you clue me in. But my advice, never trust a boggart. They can be kind, but most are full of trickery and lies."

I hooked my arm with hers, and she led me back inside. "Will I find others like us out in the human world?"

"Possibly. But I wouldn't focus on that." She patted my hand before moving away from me. "Live the human life for a while. Make some memories and lots of friends. Human magic is different and harder to detect, but when you find it, it will be profound. Ours is obvious, where theirs is mysteriously beautiful."

"I'm ready," I said, bouncing on my toes.

An outside door was yanked open in the distance, pulling my attention from Mimi.

"Dora, come quick! You must see this!" Paislee yelled through the house.

I looked at Mimi, and her eyes sparkled with delight. "Go, my love. Maybe you need to have a few more adventures here before you leave us."

Excitement coursed through me as I tore down the hallway and through the kitchen, swerving around the kitchen staff and nearly running into Paislee at the door.

"What is it?" I asked, breathless and holding onto the doorframe to steady myself.

"Those clones." A grin stretched across her face. "I mean, those faceless people... He built them from something, used power from an underground force."

I raked my fingers through my hair. "You're speaking in riddles, Pais. Spill it."

The field on the side of the estate had completely transformed into a bustling town of dark and light fairies. The land had always been a wonderland hidden from humans, aside from the few selected by Ryker to work as staff members. But he had craved the human experience and had used Mom's life force to create a reality separate from the other enchanted beings. His lifestyle as a human had been luxurious, filled with lavish travels and gifts, dancing and parties that lasted for days, and wealth beyond measure. All provided by Mom's magic. His greed knew no bounds.

The human staff wouldn't return any time soon. Mimi had mentioned in passing that their memories would fade like dreams, vanishing into the void between worlds. Should the fairies choose to open the portal to the human town again, only the chosen would have those memories restored. The logic seemed twisted and elusive. But here, in the place where the trees listened and the shadows danced just out of sight, sense was something entirely different.

Perhaps when I crossed into their world, I would understand why the fae had to be hidden, even from those who had been trusted to serve us for all these years.

"The underground tunnels." Paislee pulled on my hand. "Come with me. It's like nothing I have ever seen before."

I tugged on my shoes and followed her down the cobblestone pathway, waving at some of the new faces that turned to watch us. The fairy folks hadn't all been enthusiastic about our return, but most had been welcoming. There was a long history with my family that remained a mystery, and I suspected the strange looks from a few fairies were linked to that.

Paislee skipped ahead of me, twirling and dancing and saying hello to everyone she passed, oblivious to the few sneers. But I noticed them. And they knew I was watching.

It wouldn't stop me from leaving. I had to explore, ever if only for a few months. When I returned, I would face whatever tainted our family's reputation.

"Come, come." Paislee waved at me from nearly a half block away.

Jersey stood with her, sporting a pair of dark sunglasses.

"Should we really be going into the underground tunnels?" I asked, discomfort from the stares making me more eager to begin my journey.

"You won't want to miss this before you leave." Paislee dragged me forward and down the pathway toward the door.

I hadn't returned since the day I had helped Ryker escape. A shiver raced down my spine when the door came into view. This was a trek down memory lane I had never wanted to take again. But the elation on Paislee's face kept pushing me along.

The path and doorway had been cleared of the overgrowth of vegetation, and instead, massive trees with sprinkles of flowers adorned the entrance. Jersey pulled the wooden door open, and the light inside brightened the threshold.

Paislee disappeared inside, followed by Jersey. I held the door frame and inched inside. The tunnel traveled in both directions, but to the right was where I had always met with Ryker. Paislee skipped in the same direction, beckoning for me to follow.

Nothing was different inside, aside from the silence. I searched for any signs of Ryker or his men, even though I knew they were gone. If any of them hadn't been an illusion and had not perished in our fight, they remained in a world that no longer existed for us.

Paislee veered off to her left, down another tunnel. I picked up my pace and passed Jersey, falling into step with my sister. She reached for me, and we intertwined our fingers, swinging our arms between us like we had as children.

"What did you find?" I squeezed her hand.

The tunnel curved to the right, and if my sense of direction was correct, we were traveling toward the grate in the garden.

"You have to see it to believe it." She dropped my hand

and turned to check on Jersey, walking backward with a small dance in her step. "It was below our feet, and we never knew it. Even Mom couldn't figure out where they came from."

We had never talked about the blood I had stolen from them, and I wasn't ready to disclose that part of Ryker's plan. My pulse quickened when the outside light caught my attention. The tunnel ended, and a vast room opened for us. My jaw dropped from the sparkle illuminating from the rocks.

Paislee waved her arm forward, excitement taking over her features. "See! They have filled up this room and did not exist before Ryker was imprisoned here. No one can explain them."

I moved through the room, careful not to touch the red stones protruding from the walls, ceiling, and floor. My gaze drifted upward to where the ceiling curved, then to where the grate was embedded into the stone.

"What is this place?" I asked as I crouched to inspect a large gemstone near my feet.

"Mom claims it leads to other fae communities. Each door accesses civilizations around the world, but access was restricted when Ryker siphoned her magic for the first time." Paislee kneeled beside me. "They couldn't chance his influence or power to filter into their lives."

A knot festered in my stomach. "Can't blame them. I would do the same."

My fingers grazed the rock. It brightened from my touch, and across the way, a figure similar to mine emerged. Its faceless head turned in our direction. I fell backward with a gasp, and the figure disappeared in a puff of smoke.

"Careful, Dora." Jersey stood over us with a pained expression on his face. "Ryker summoned hundreds of these with a mere thought. Your power is far more superior."

"But what are they?" I scrambled to my feet, wiping off the dirt from my pants.

"We don't know yet." Paislee brushed her hands together as she rose next to me, her gaze never leaving the spot the figure had emerged from. "The red gems, the intense energy, and those faceless clones all started with something Ryker did. But without him here, we might never find our answers."

Terror gripped my chest. This wasn't Ryker. This happened because of me—because I had stolen blood from my family and mixed it together. I couldn't find the courage to divulge that information.

I backed away from the gems and into the corridor just outside of the room.

"We shouldn't be here." I pushed my palms against my cheeks and shook my head. "In fact, we should block anyone from having access until we know what we are dealing with."

Paislee stopped next to me and patted my shoulder. "We won't pry too much while you're away. Maybe when you return, you and I can dig into the real elements from the gems and pinpoint their origin. I'm in no hurry to build an army." Her laughter echoed around the room, and the red gems brightened from the sound.

My mouth turned dry when ghostly figures slid into focus. Jersey's jaw ticked, and he muttered something under his breath before throwing his hand out toward the room. The figures melted away.

I gulped and met Jersey's gaze. He lifted his brows at me but only shook his head before walking away.

"Brilliant idea. I think blocking access is the best course of action," Jersey said as he grabbed Paislee's hand and linked it with his elbow. "A mystery that can be solved after Pandora returns."

Heat crept up my cheeks as shame washed over me. He must have suspected my deceit, but his silence meant something I couldn't quite pinpoint without speaking to him. And I had no intention of doing that. I walked behind them, grateful to put that room in my past for now. Maybe it was better to keep my secret and allow Paislee the time to grow in her powers before we explored ways to defuse whatever lay in the tunnels.

I held no answers, only a hollow yearning for a normal life, a final breath of sunlight before surrendering to the shadows of magic. If that made me selfish, then so be it. I would wear the sin like a crown.

For now.

MESSAGE FROM THE AUTHOR

I stopped writing the second half of 2023 and most of 2024. My ten-year relationship with an unhappy, never satisfied, always finding fault with anybody but him, was crumbling. And for reasons I couldn't fully understand, my heart shattered. I knew it had to end. He had worn me down to a shell of who I once was, and I ached to have my light back. But the thought of losing him petrified me.

Then, in the dead of winter, he walked out. The thick falling snow swallowed him whole before I could even register what had happened. From that moment on, it became easier. Even when he showed up at our home every few days to pick up more of his belongings and hurling fresh or recycled accusations at me.

I clung to weekly therapy sessions and wrapped myself in self-care and the people who truly loved me. I slowly untangled myself from the web of manipulation he had spun. His games had been a way to control and diminish me, so he could feel bigger, stronger. He stole my light, and when I finally shut him out, he felt the loss.

He came running.

But I stood my ground and blocked him from gaining access again.

Today, I am whole again.

I tell you this condensed story to explain my absence and to give you a small peek into why I wrote this story the way I did. I am grateful to be free of the abuse that I endured and it's a blessing each day when I wake feeling hope and happiness once again.

This story is a way for my experience to speak to those going through the same or similar trials and I hope it reaches the ones who need it the most. I really do see you. I understand the heartache you are experiencing or have experienced. And healing is possible.

To those who helped me mold this story, thank you!

Angie and her team at Novel Nurse Editing, you once again have been fantastic to work with and I appreciate the feedback you have provided to round out the sharp edges of this story. It's always a pleasure to work with you.

To the team at GetCovers, I adore this book cover. Thank you for the quick responses and creative imagination provided.

Thank you to everyone who has supported me, especially during my transition to a new and brighter life. Michelle, Rachael, Crystal, Courtney, Vivian, and Melissa, when I needed each of you, there was no hesitation in showing up and holding space for me. You are all my sisters and I appreciate and love you all.

To Gary, thank you for walking into my office that day.

Our laughs and connection have meant the world to me, and I am looking forward to many more days like the ones we have spent together. Your pride in my writing and the way you talk about me to others, warms my heart and brightens my days. Thank you for being you.

To my children, I love you. Always and forever, to infinity and beyond. Thank you for loving me back and supporting me in my wild imagination. And to Juni Bug, my sweet, adorable granddaughter, you are my angel, my little doodlebug and I hope you enjoy my stories one day.

There are still so many stories within me, waiting to be shared with the world. I will return soon, with the new tales spun and woven just for you.

BOOKS BY NIKI LIVINGSTON

Infernal Crystals

Shadow of the Serpent Curse (Prequel)
Descendant of the Serpent Queen
Guardians of the Serpent Empire
Watchers of the Serpent Prisoner - TBA

Theia's Moons Series

Eyes Wide Shut
Enyo's Warrior
Protectors of the Stars
Guardian

The Chaos Awakened Saga

Marked Chaos
Expanded Chaos
Transformed Chaos

Novels

Be My Leprechaun
Daughters of a Dark Fairy

Novellas

Wrong Side of the Mirror

Novelettes

A Web Through Time
Wicked Heart
Wicked Soul
Jolly Old Monster
Unable to Wake

ABOUT THE AUTHOR

International Bestselling Author Niki Livingston writes tales of fantasy worlds filled with magic, mysticism, and mystery.

When she's not busy writing enchanting stories of diverse women rising in their power and strength, she spends her time walking her rescue puppy, quieting her mind with meditation and yoga, diving into the newest books of Veronica Roth and Anne Bishop, and binge-watching anything fantasy, sci-fi, or a thrilling adventure.

For all her latest releases and updates, subscribe to Niki Livingston's newsletter! www.NikiLivingston.com